RAGE IN
ABUNDANCE

ALSO BY ARLETTE LEES

Angel Doll
Hollywood Heat
Midnight Rain

TALES OF ABUNDANCE

Murder in Abundance
Trouble in Abundance

RAGE IN ABUNDANCE

ARLETTE LEES

WILDSIDE PRESS

Published by Wildside Press LLC.
wildsidepress.com | bcmystery.com

CHAPTER 1

HUSBAND NUMBER FOUR

Duane Calhoun was fresh out of the pen with an old score to settle, stole a car and set out for Abundance, Wisconsin. His luck had changed years before when his wife, a stubborn red-head, realized he wasn't exactly who he pretended to be. Then again, who is?

After a few years, when her passion for his sexual prowess began to wane, she dismantled their relationship one insult at a time.

"I don't want you behind the bar. I'm tired of tripping over your feet."

"What do you want from me?" he said, glancing around for someone to take up his cause.

"You might try getting a job," said Gladys. "Standing on a woman's shoulders does not make a man taller."

The remark cut to the bone and his love for the woman he called Red, turned into something darker and colder. Still, he had a comfortable situation and didn't want to lose it.

A man in a John Deere cap said: "Don't be so hard on him, Gladys. He's better looking than your last three husbands."

That got a laugh and he joined in to cover his angst.

Gladys made Cal return the key to the cigarette machine, made him pay for his drinks. It was humiliating for a man whose wife owned a bar.

Gladys remembered the night Cal stepped off the Greyhound bus with nothing but a cardboard suitcase, a deck of marked cards and a Saturday night special tucked beneath his folded shirts. He had an easy manner and mesmerizing blue eyes. A couple drinks, a little conversation and her over-active hormones screwed up her life one more time.

At first Duane had been helpful and charming. They always are until they get their shoes under your bed and their fingers in your piggy bank. When Duane talked about his past, he couldn't keep his stories straight, said he'd been a real estate associate in Chicago the same time he was Car Salesman of the Year in Detroit. The inconsistencies were adding up.

When Cal went from dipping into her wallet to raiding the till, she hired a P.I. named Dirk Denham to look into Duane's past. Gladys wanted out.

Denham found there had been a former Mrs. Calhoun, maiden name, Margie Downs. Big deal. Gladys didn't care. Then Denham found a Marriage Certificate out of Milwaukee, but no record of a Divorce Decree or Death Certificate in any jurisdiction. This got her attention. There had to be one or the other unless Duane boogied in the night to avoid divorce proceedings or ended their relationship with a bullet.

Was Calhoun capable of that degree of violence? She wasn't sure.

A wife he'd never divorced put an interesting slant on things now that she wanted him gone. If he was still legally married to Margie Downs—and he couldn't prove otherwise—their own marriage was invalid. There would be no splitting of marital assets, no expensive court battles. Gladys was a fool for men, but she was nobody's fool when it came to money.

Her P.I. broadened his investigation. The neighbors who still lived on the block remembered Margie as a young lady who was always *walking into doors*, new bruises replacing the old. Everyone knew what was going on, but no one wanted to cross Duane Calhoun.

When the landlord, 55 year old Joel Bender—a soft-spoken, respectable type who lived across town from his apartment building—didn't receive his rent, he called the Calhoun's number. The phone had been disconnected, the apartment vacant. He found Margie's raided purse on a chair—no money in the wallet, no driver's license, address book or family pictures—no way to contact family or friends. Mr. Bender had a bad feeling when he saw her makeup on the bathroom counter, her clothes in the closet, and no items indicating a man had lived there. He had quite a story to tell Private Investigator Denham.

Every big city had its share of missing women and unless they came from prominent families the police didn't want to be bothered. An adult had a right to disappear without notifying anyone, so he was told. Be patient, she'll eventually resurface like *that kind of woman* always does. Mr. Bender was offended and left. He stored Margie's things in his attic, but she never returned to retrieve them.

In the following 20 years Margie had left no paper trail—no credit cards—no bank accounts—no traffic violations. Either she'd changed her identity or dropped into a shallow grave.

Gladys and Calhoun had already talked about a fair divorce settlement, although they each had their own definition of fair. When she threatened to go to the police with the private detective's report, he vanished like he had before, this time with nothing to show for the years he and Red had spent together running the bar. Maybe he wasn't perfect, but in the beginning he'd loved Red deeply and at one time he knew she'd loved him back.

Several months later Gladys talked to Milwaukee P.D. about Margie Downs, but was unable to generate any interest. Too many years had gone by. There were no leads to follow. Margie Downs had become a ghost.

One detective, however, had taken notes. His name was Fred Ferguson. In the days following Gladys's visit, the mystery of Miss Downs was like a fly that kept buzzing his nose. He located Duane in a local jail on a bad check charge and paid him a visit.

Calhoun said Margie dumped him for another man. He had no photo of her. He didn't know any of her relatives. He couldn't remember if she was a blonde or a brunette.

"Her DOB?" asked Ferguson.

"Not a clue."

"Why do you think she left her purse and clothes behind?" he asked.

"She was forgetful," said Calhoun.

"Would you consent to a lie detector test so we can eliminate you as a suspect?"

"A suspect in what? Not having cuddly feelings toward the woman who dumped me? Gladys is a scorned woman out to destroy me. She's sent you on a wild goose chase."

Cal called for the jailer and returned to his cell.

* * * *

Years later while doing a stretch in the state pen for embezzlement, Cal obsessed over his mistreatment by Red. She'd cheated him out of his marital assets and stirred up that old Margie thing. He'd never been the same since. He gave up on himself. He got in trouble. He dreamed about the life he might have had, if only—

Since then, his body had become victim to his addictions, his blue eyes having turned a cloudy grey, his photo-perfect face, ten miles of bad road.

A sharp pain twisted beneath Calhoun's rib cage causing him to swerve onto the shoulder of the road. Lost in fantasies of revenge, he'd forgotten he was driving a car. He fish-tailed back into his lane and straightened out the wheel.

Just recently his complexion had taken on an orange pallor and the area beneath his right rib cage felt tender to the touch. The prison doctor detected spots on his liver. He didn't need a medical degree to figure that one out. The only time the pain subsided was when he drank himself into unconsciousness.

With only six months left on his sentence, the parole board cut him loose. After all, how much trouble can a dying man get into?"

Cal passed a road sign. Abundance was still a few hours up the road. By then it would be dark and he'd be ready to dole out a little overdue justice.

CHAPTER 2

BROKEN TIES

Seasoned calf roper and bronc rider Dyce Dean Jackson, stood behind the stock pens at the end of Rodeo Sunday. The Rotary Club of Abundance had sponsored the first event on this year's summer circuit filling the town coffers with a much needed infusion of cash. The event was over, the stands deserted, the booted and spurred contestants preparing to move on to the next venue after a few beers at the local watering holes.

At 45, Dyce was a ruggedly handsome man with just the right amount of silver at his temples. Tall, well-muscled and square-jawed, he was often mistaken for the Marlboro Man, mustache, cigarettes and all.

Coby Dillon, his young protégé, gave Dyce a friendly fist bump. In the three years of their partnership Coby had gone from a green kid to a competent bullrider. Dyce liked things the way they'd been, the kid relying on his road smarts and rodeo expertize. Tonight was their last event as partners. Coby was settling down with Brielle, and Dyce was odd guy out.

"Thanks to you, I've had the time of my life," said Coby, his young face beaming. When I'm old and gray I'll look back on these years as my coming of age. It's been a pleasure partnering with you my friend."

Dyce smiled congenially, secretly hoping the girl would dump Coby or that her parents would rein in their beautiful young daughter so things could go back the way they used to be. Instead, the romance had deepened and matured, squeezing Dyce out of the equation.

For three years it had been Dyce and Coby. Now it was Coby and Brielle, the quiet, dark-eyed girl from Frenchman Wood, who'd busted up their partnership with innocent finality. The minute Coby heard her lilting French accent, his heart melted like a snowball in a hot frying pan.

"So, you're ducking out on me," said Dyce, pushing the words past the ache in his throat. "Without rodeo what are you going to do for money?"

"I start work at the hardware store on Monday. Brielle will be living with me and Grandma out on Dane Road."

Today Coby had ridden Devil's Trumpet to the 8-second buzzer with the grace and agility of an adagio dancer. The bull had never been ridden before and Coby became an instant hometown hero, fancy trophy buckle and all. Another year and he'd have been raking in big bucks. Now he was throwing it all away for peanuts.

Dyce opened his mouth to speak but Coby knew what was coming and waved him off.

"No more questions," he laughed. "I don't want you worrying about me anymore."

When Coby walked away Dyce discovered the kid had tucked $200.00 into the pocket of his jeans jacket, compensation for Dyce's poor performance in the arena that afternoon.

Although the money was given in good will, it was humiliating to be so broke that he couldn't turn it down. He considered making some bullshit statement about paying it back, but Coby was already starting his truck.

A chilly wind blew down from the north carrying with it a bank of dark clouds. Wisconsin weather was like that. It could turn on a dime. Rain would be a blessing after the suffocating heat of the day. Dyce took out his bandanna and wiped the dust from his forehead. As he moved toward his truck the sciatic nerve in his bad leg zinged with pain. He was no longer ranked among the best in his class, but he was still good enough to last one more season, bad leg and all.

Dyce tapped a smoke from his pack and scraped a kitchen match on the sole of his boot the way his daddy used to do. He'd lost count of how many broncs his dad had ridden or how tall he'd been without his big ten-gallon hat—just the match and the cigarette and how tobacco smoke and sweat clung to his old man's clothes. They'd lived out of an old Ford truck as they'd travelled the west from one two-bit rodeo to the next. It was an exciting life for a kid who couldn't sit still in a classroom.

A lifetime ago D. D. Jackson, Sr. was fatally gored in a dusty town near the Mexican border and Dyce's life was turned upside down. At fifteen he stepped into his dad's cowboy boots and wore them until the soles came loose. With no mother in his life, even when he was small, his only home was the rodeo. He keyed up the Ford and headed down the road to the next event. Both he and Coby had lost their parents at a young age and their mutual loss had formed a strong bond.

The light was fading and the pretty female deputy with the dark chestnut hair was getting ready to chain the main entrance for the night. He remembered a time when ladies carried babies instead of guns and it made him feel as if the world he'd once known was passing him by.

The deputy looked toward the back of the bullpens and motioned for the last stragglers to wind it up. She'd covered at least five miles working security in boots that felt tighter with every step. Dyce had watched her break up a fight between two men twice her size. The men ended up shaking hands and going their separate ways. He had to admit that she was good at what she did.

Coby was first out of the lot with his shiny trophy buckle and the remaining $800.00 of his winnings. He turned north in the direction of Frenchman Wood, his horse trailer clamped and chained to the hitch. The Wood was a thick expanse of forest, swampland and unpaved roads, sparsely populated by French families who minded their own business and lived by their own rules.

As the sky darkened and Coby's tail lights faded in the distance, Dyce had an epiphany. He tucked the $200.00 in his wallet, checked his horse trailer and starting his engine. Maybe there was still time to talk sense to the kid. Girls were dime a dozen, even pretty ones. They came and went, but rodeo was real and so was their friendship.

He threw the truck into gear and floored the gas pedal. The tires squealed as he shot past the deputy. She jumped back to keep from getting clocked in the head by his side mirror, the blowback flipping her hat to the ground. Gunpowder, Dyce's 12 year old roping horse thumped against the side of the trailer as he swung onto the road.

When he glanced in his rear view the deputy had retrieved her hat and was writing down his license number. He felt bad for cutting it so close but relieved that he'd be out of state within hours.

Looking back, Dyce wished he'd never followed Coby into Frenchman Wood, but he didn't know then that things would turn out the way they did.

CHAPTER 3

LIFE ON THE LITTLE PAPOOSE

My significant other, Frank "Frack" Telusky and I are deputy sheriffs out of the small substation on Main Street. We live in unwedded bliss in a big cream-colored Victorian on Cedar Street overlooking the town square with its mature shade trees, acrobatic squirrels and deep green grass.

Me? I'm Robely Danner, Robely, as in row your boat, not rob your bank. I'm just tall enough that when I say, *Please step out of your car, sir,* the driver usually complies, the badge on my belt and the gun in my holster providing an extra element of authority.

Frack picked up his nickname working oil-fracking operations in North Dakota after a long stint as M.P. in the Marines. He quit fracking when an industrial-induced earthquake caused local drinking water to ignite at the touch of a match. The men working the rig were warned to keep their mouths shut or find work elsewhere. Frack quit and returned to Abundance after half a lifetime's absence from the farm life he'd known as a kid. We were short a deputy at the substation and I was short a man in my life. Not that I can't go it on my own. I just figure a double bed is happier with two people in it—well, two people and a big friendly dog named Fargo.

Frack with his military police background was quickly hired onto the force and we partnered up both professionally and personally. I'm 29. He's older as evidenced by the white strands winding through his sandy hair. He has a hard, whippy frame, sinewy arms and deep blue-green eyes. He is, by nature, kind and considerate. He can also be tough as leather if the situation demands. After surviving a rough childhood, he's my safe haven, my soft place to fall. Using my fingers and toes I count the years that separate us and have one toe left. You can do the math—or not.

The woods behind our house runs a half mile to a bend in the Little Papoose River as it flows out of town into rolling pastures and endless fields of feed corn and soy beans. In the backyard the branches of an apple tree lean over the roof of a potting shed. There's a good-size garden plot, an old-fashioned clothes line and a row of sunflowers nodding their bushy heads beside the garage wall.

Out front the roots of a monkey puzzle tree raise a corner of sidewalk just enough to catch the toe of the unwary who are glued to their Smart Phones. We've seen our share of skinned knees, tumbling school books and communication devices skitter across the concrete.

The population of Abundance has slipped from 5000 in its lumber-rich days to a little under 1000 at the last census. Although the town's not dead, it's definitely on life support. The saw mill has gone the way of the movie house and Five and Dime, and if it weren't for our bubble-top water tower, few people driving the main highway would know our town is tucked into the landscape beyond the river.

Several houses in town, some of them belonging to my neighbors, are in foreclosure. For Rent signs fade in half the store windows on the one block business district, the result of a crippled economy and a Wal*Mart in a nearby town that challenges local establishments with rock-bottom prices. Our young high school graduates gravitate to the city for jobs and our senior citizens bloom where they were planted.

We've managed to retain a grocery store with three cramped aisles, a Gas and Go, feed store, hardware store, tractor outlet and the Bluebird Café among a handful of other small struggling businesses. On the wrong side of the tracks are the towering grain elevators, Bubba's Biker Bar, Lucky's Pawn Shop and a few scattered trailers sitting ankle-deep in mud in spring-time and knee-deep in snow in winter. The right side of the tracks is lined with both big and small Victorian houses with squeaky porch swings and frosted glass ovals in the front doors, others with a touch of stained glass framing the front room windows.

We have two bars in addition to Bubba's, Gladys's on the main highway and The Edge of Town, classy as hell with red leather booths and an antique mahogany bar that came around The Horn over 200 years ago. The water-ing holes are noisy and packed on Saturday nights, our one church quiet and half empty on Sunday mornings.

Like all small towns everyone knows who's on food stamps, has DWI's or has lost their shirts at the Hochunk Casino in Wittenburg. The phone lines might go down in a blizzard, but the local grapevine is fully operative in all weather. A complaint to the station might be anything from Oxyco-done or underage girls being peddled out the back door of Bubba's, to a neighbor complaining about a noisy leaf blower on a lazy Sunday morning.

My mother is Gladys Calhoun. Yes, Gladys of Gladys's Bar. Four times married and divorced—or so I hear—her establishment sits along the high-way in the mosquito zone above the banks of the Little Papoose River. It's a family bar where mid-life and elderly couples with bad livers and COPD feel at home. It's also the cowboy's favorite hangout during the Abundance Invitational Rodeo.

As a youngster I was virtually nameless, known only as *the girl who lives above the bar.* It set me apart from other kids in town whose parents had dairy herds or worked at Hillshire Farms. In my upstairs bedroom I drifted off to the click of billiard balls, leather dice cups thumping against the bar and records played on a 1940's Wurlitzer, the kind with bubbling red and yellow tubes running up the sides. Gladys keeps a Derringer beneath the cash drawer and a can of bear spray at arm's length. She's had a troubled life of failed marriages and one night stands, but seems tough enough to handle whatever comes down the pike.

I was not so lucky. Fear ran through my childhood like a rusty razor blade. It was after last call when the doors were bolted that I trembled in my bed. The Wurlitzer would go quiet and two pairs of footsteps would stagger up the stairs. The racket of the bar was more comforting than the silences that followed. I never knew what was coming next. It's something I don't dwell on, but it still haunts my dreams from time to time.

By the time I was born, Gladys had a rap sheet longer than her arm, starting with petty crimes committed by a rebellious teenage drop-out who ran with the bad boys and drank Jack Daniels under the bridge. It's doubtful she was ever ready for motherhood, but I came along and there was no un-ringing that bell.

Gladys gave me her maiden name, Danner, while she kept Calhoun, the name of husband number four. The only man she never wed was the father of her only child, yours truly.

Gladys refuses to discuss my biological father. She won't tell me his name or where I might find him. My birth certificate lists my father as "unknown" which I know is a lie. Gladys's sister Lorene told me he was a Frenchman down from Canada, a lumberjack with two fingers missing from his left hand. She said he ditched Gladys when she wouldn't stop sleeping around and driving drunk with me in the car. For three or four years he tried to make things work. He finally gave up and left. He wanted to keep me, but in those days it was almost impossible to take a child from her mother, especially if you weren't an American citizen.

I don't remember him feature for feature, but I knew he loved me. I remember his gentle touch, the soft wool of his plaid shirts and the smell of pine and wood smoke in his hair. I still feel his presence in ways I can't explain. I remember that his brown eyes were the same color as mine.

When Gladys found out that Lorene had confided in me, tempers flared and Lorene moved away. To this day I check men's hands for missing fingers—when I go to farm auctions and gun shows and attend the World Lumberjack Competition in Hayward. My father may never resurface. I may never find him, but I'll never stop searching.

* * * *

I limp up the stairs to my bedroom in my cowboy boots and Stetson. The boots fit quite well when I put them on this morning but after a day in the heat they're a couple sizes smaller than my feet.

Frack's been waiting for me at the window. He tosses my hat on the dresser and spins me in a circle, unclips my barrette and fluffs out my thick auburn hair with his fingers.

"I knew my girl was in there somewhere," he says, holding my face between his hands and giving me a kiss. "It's almost dark. I thought you'd run off with that handsome Brazilian bullrider."

"He already has a wife and two mistresses. I'd have to book a year in advance."

"Then you'll be mine a while longer."

"A *forever* while," I say. "

He holds me at arm's length.

"Your nose is peeling. It must have been murder out there in this humidity."

"At least there were no serious injuries this year. There was one scuffle but it didn't amount to much,"

I collapse on the bedspread and Frack wrestles with my boots."

"What did you do, glue them on?" he says, working them off inch by slow painful inch and tossing them into the closet with a thud. He massages my burning feet and painfully bunched toes.

"That feels so good I could die," I say. "So how was *your* day?"

"Big Mike put me on traffic. You know how dangerous it gets when muscle-trucks and horse trailers mix with Amish buggies."

I think of the guy in the pickup who almost knocked my head off, but decide not to mention it.

"Mike was catching up on paperwork this afternoon. When I checked in with him I could hear the fan whirring ever so coolly in the background," says Frack.

Undersheriff, Big Mike Oxenburg is our immediate superior. We three make a good team. He prefers the position of desk jockey, while Frack and I enjoy being in the field. He's put on a few extra pounds while his nose was stuck in the donut box, but Mike is tough as nails under fire.

Sheriff/Coroner, Ernie Brooker is our Big Boss. He sits in his private office at the morgue in the county seat. He's top man on the totem pole, but we don't see much of him unless something big is going on or there's an opportunity for a photo op.

I push up the window overlooking The Square. The air has cooled, the wind is up and the sky has grown dark with storm clouds. The filmy white curtains blow inward and Frack stands behind me, the top of my head fitting neatly under his chin. Leaves flutter in the wind and the street lamp goes on across the street.

"The house feels so empty without Fargo," I say. "Dr. Crane is giving him the works this time: boosters, dental cleaning, nail clipping, flea bath and a fluff dry."

"A fluff? The life of a dog isn't what it was when I was growing up on the farm," says Frack.

"Nothing is the way it used to be—except us."

When Frack goes downstairs to turn off the lights, I shed my western duds and step into the shower. The sky flashes gold and the first rumble of thunder rolls across the sky.

CHAPTER 4

TROUBLE IN FRENCHMAN WOOD

Coby cruised north on the two-lane leading to Frenchman Wood. He rolled his shoulders to work out the kinks. He loved the twilight hour when a purple veil dropped over the cornfields and pastures. He inhaled the scent of pine and impending rain. He was free for the first time in three years. No 8 second buzzers. No greasy burgers and bitter coffee consumed on the run. He was ready for his new life with the girl he adored.

An arrow of lightning shot through the darkening sky. He could smell ozone in the air. Rain would be a welcome blessing after the dust and humidity of the arena. Love was in bloom. Life was good.

With only a few miles to go before the turnoff to Frenchman Wood, he fantasized about his future with Brielle. He imagined his fingers running through her long, silky hair—hair as black as night—her heart beating against his chest. He loved the satiny texture of her skin and the spark of playfulness in her dark brown eyes.

His last three summers had been dominated by dust, heat and the sour sweat of man and beast. Sure, the easy camaraderie of his rodeo buddies had been a blast, but he needed a grounded life. He was a homebody at heart.

He'd been driving about thirty minutes when high beams from a vehicle behind him flashed in his rear view. He snapped out of his daydream and gripped the wheel more tightly. He had Chili, a ten thousand dollar quarter horse mare in the trailer behind him and he couldn't afford a careless driver climbing up his tail pipe. He waved a hand out the window to indicate it was safe to pass, but the vehicle stayed glued to his tail. Coby shaded his eyes against the glare and squinted into the side mirror.

"What the—? Dyce! Sonofabitch!" he whispered, even though he wasn't much for cussing. Hadn't they already said their good-byes? He liked Dyce, enjoyed the three years they'd partnered together, but that was behind him now, or so he thought. He couldn't tolerate another day of his ex-partners constant mothering. He was his own man now.

Dyce tapped his horn, politely at first. Coby ignored him. *Please, please, just go away.* Dyce tapped the horn again, this time more insistently.

Damned if Coby was going to pull over and have the same conversation they'd had half an hour ago. He was meeting Brielle at the bridge over Lost Squaw Creek and he didn't want the intrusion of a third party ruining their special moment.

As he drove, the endless fields of corn and flowering pastures gave way to thickening forest. The air was heavy with the spicy scent of evergreen. Paget Corner with its worn steps and unpainted wood siding came into view. The elderly proprietors of the small grocery store, Jim and Tim Paget, sat in their rocking chairs watching the sky, waiting for rain. Paget Corner was the swinging door between the regular world and the more reclusive Frenchman Wood.

There was a hand-scrawled sign in the window: *Des Cuisses de Grenouille*—frog legs. A great delicacy he'd only recently been introduced to. Frog legs were among the first words Brielle had taught him in French. As he tried pronouncing them, they had broken out in laughter. "Everything in French sounds like, *I want to make love to you*," he'd said.

"Of course. It's the language of love. But, until I'm out from beneath my parent's roof, we wait. Out of respect. You understand, right?"

"Yes, out of respect," he agreed. She'd kissed him on the cheek. It had been a hard commitment to honor, but honor it they had.

The Paget brothers waved and Coby finger-tapped the brim of his cowboy hat.

With Chili trailered behind the truck Coby took the turn into Frenchman Wood slowly. Once he was on the dirt track there was no way to avoid the ridges, roots and ruts that promised to loosen the joints and sinews of the sturdiest vehicle. He looked over his shoulder. Dyce had turned into the road behind him.

He's like gum stuck to my shoe, thought Coby. *I'll never get rid of him.*

Maybe Dyce wanted to thank him for the money. It wasn't necessary. Coby still had funds enough to last until his first paycheck from the hardware store. He decided the quickest way to get rid of him was to go with the flow.

After ten minutes driving deeper into the sylvan gloom, Brielle's driveway came up on his right. Her parents had never extended their hospitality, so he'd never driven up to the house. The Broussard's didn't forbid Brielle from seeing him, but he wasn't brought into the family circle either. He wasn't French. He didn't know the language and culture. He wasn't even Catholic. In their eyes he was an unsuitable match for their only daughter.

He drove another half mile and pulled over just short of Lost Squaw Bridge. Upstream the creek broadened into a bayou where waterlilies folded their petals for the night, and an occasional fish jumped among the reeds.

Stones popped beneath Dyce's tires as he pulled in behind him. Coby turned off the ignition. Dyce did the same. They met half way between the trucks.

"Hey, man," said Coby. "What's up?"

"Why didn't you pull over?" said Dyce.

Coby didn't feel he owed him an explanation, but he wanted to keep the peace.

"I'm meeting someone and I'm running late. I thought we'd already said our good-byes."

"Not entirely."

"What is that supposed to mean?" said Coby, glancing at the gathering clouds.

"Just hear me out. It won't take but a minute."

Lightning crackled through a thick bank of clouds and a marble of rain hit Coby's hat. Unless Brielle left soon, she'd be caught in the rain. He wanted to drive back and meet her when she reached the bottom of her driveway, but first he had to get rid of Dyce.

* * * *

In a clearing cut from the woods stood a house constructed of cedar logs. It had sheltered generations of Broussards ever since the French were driven out of Canada for refusing to pledge allegiance to the English Crown. Many of the exiled migrated to New Orleans where French was spoken and the state was governed by French Law. Others, like the Broussards, relocated to Wisconsin where the French had established the first permanent settlement in the state in Green Bay back in 1761.

Adjacent to the house was an unpainted barn, a scattering of outbuildings for chickens and pigs, a large garden plot and extensive acreage tended only by nature's hand.

Pierre 'Pete' Broussard, his nineteen year old son Archer, and three neighbor men sat on the porch steps drinking mugs of strong whiskey-laced coffee and smoking black cheroots. They spoke in lowered voices, laughing from time to time at a memory or joke.

When the family hounds saw rifles leaning against the porch railing they rubbed against the men's knees in anticipation of the hunt. Pete looked at the sky. If the rain held off like the weatherman predicted, they might have time to poach a buck or tree a raccoon before they got washed out of the woods.

When conversation turned to The Rivettes, they spoke quietly, the Rivettes being Pete's closest neighbors and oldest adversaries. Because the Broussard's property was accessed from Bridge Road and the Rivette's entered theirs from an old logging road beyond Paget Corner, they seldom crossed paths.

Both families suffered heavy casualties in the Whiskey Wars of the 1930's and memories on both sides ran long and hard. They hung on to the grudge despite the fact that only the most elderly members of the family remembered the names of those who had fallen to the violence. There hadn't been an 'incident' in some time but hostilities were hiding a cat's-scratch beneath the surface.

"I haven't seen Devil Rivette since his bout with the flu last winter," said a man named Remy, who wore a traditional French knit cap.

"Why, you miss him?" said Pete, and they all laughed.

"At least he hasn't busted up our still lately," said Archer, the only Broussard son allowed to sit in on adult conversation.

"Talk is he isn't well enough to tend the still."

"He used to cover these hills like a Billy goat," said Beau, the youngest of the three visitors. "You never see him at the juke anymore either. I can't deny the man played a mean fiddle. That's where he got his name when he was just thirteen years old. Someone said, *that young de Roye plays like the devil, don't he?* From that day on he became Devil Rivette."

"Even with her arthritis Sabine seems to get around, what little we see of her these days," said Cheney, buffing the stock of his gun with a piece of sheep skin. The old Devil is bad enough but she's half blind and plumb crazy."

"Crazy like a fox," said Remy.

They chatted on as a light snapped on in an upstairs bedroom where Brielle was packing her suitcase. Her 9 year old twin brothers Anton and Henri looked on as she decided which items were essential to her new life with Coby and his grandmother and which items could be left behind.

"Are you really going?" asked Anton, the bolder of the boys.

"Yes, I'm really going."

"With that rodeo fellow?" said Henri.

"Yes, with Coby Dillon, the rodeo fellow."

"Why?"

"When you're older you won't have to ask."

"What the heck is a Dillon?" said Anton? "It's always been the Broussards, Chereaus and Rochons. It's been that way forever. Besides, Archer says you promised to marry Charlie Chereau."

Brielle felt a small twinge of pain beneath her heart. "Charlie is a nice man, but you can't make a forever promise when you're six years old. Besides Charlie married someone else."

"At least Charlie's one of us," said Anton, "and his wife's been dead three years now. Suzette says she's sunk her hook and all she has to do is reel him in. Pete told me if ever a girl was hot to trot it was Cousin Suzette."

"Don't ever repeat that, Anton," she said firmly.

"Even if it's true?"

"Especially if it's true. It's not a nice thing to say."

It still hurts when she thinks of Charlie marrying Julie, even though she was only 11 at the time. When Brielle was in grammar school she'd promised to marry Charlie when she grew up, but he'd never promised her back so it didn't count.

"Will you come back and visit?" asked Henri.

She leaned down and tousled the hair on their heads. "Of course I'll visit, but not for a while. I need to get settled first."

"Who will get us up for school?" whined Henri.

"You will get yourself up like grown men."

"Who's going to gather the eggs? You can't walk away from your flock."

"The chickens belong to you two now. You can split the egg money and start saving for that pony you want."

Anton looked at Henri and grinned. Maybe her leaving wasn't so bad after all.

The stairs creaked and mother Adele stepped into the room. She had the take-charge manner of a woman used to hard work. She was tall and straight as a birch tree, wore sturdy leather shoes and long skirts. A single white braid fell to her waist. Brielle was slender and tall like both of her parents, but small-boned and fine-featured.

"You boys go downstairs. I want a word with your sister."

"Oh, Mom!" they protested.

"Now!"

"You can't talk me out of this," said Brielle, when they were alone. "You were only fifteen when you married Pete and I'll be eighteen in October." She and her brothers had always called their dad Pete and no one seemed to mind. "You know how Coby and I feel about each other."

"Your dad and I were another matter. I was a Rochon. He's a Broussard. We knew what we were buying into, at least as much as one can."

"We'll only be 45 minutes away at the end of Dane Road. No reason you can't come by."

"I'll consider it."

Adele pulled a small box from her skirt pocket. She tucked it in the corner of her daughter's suitcase. "A parting gift," she said.

"What is it?"

"Inside is a card of pills. Read the box. Take them as directed."

"Why?"

"So you won't have a baby until the time is right. When you run low, call Dr. Belmont."

"Mom, we want to get *married!* All we need is parental consent."

"If things go well we'll discuss it in 6 months."

"In six months I'll be 18. I won't need your signature. What would Father Devereaux say about your being so stubborn?"

"He'd say your cowboy isn't Catholic. Give it some time. Be sure this is what you want before you jump off the deep end."

Brielle kissed her mother on the cheek, snapped her suitcase shut and tugged it off the bed. Strange how her 17 years were compressed into one small package.

"You'll need these," said Adele, handing Brielle a flashlight and umbrella.

It would be hard managing all three items now that the wind was up. "It's almost dark," said Adele. "Stay off the road. Take the path through the woods and don't aggravate the Rivettes. You know what they're like."

Brielle heard voices and looked out the window. Charlie had arrived, her once-upon-a-time fiancé when she was in the throes of serious puppy love. He was devastatingly handsome in that French backwoods way—hard-muscled, dark-haired and hazel–eyed. He partnered with Pete in the family business and also ran his own sawmill at his home on Thistle Hill.

With guns and dogs in tow, the six men disappeared into the woods in the opposite direction of the bridge. At least she wouldn't run into them on her way to meet Coby.

She knew Pete and Charlie had done a run a couple nights before, but never knew exactly where they went or who they did business with. She always laid awake until she heard the vehicle pull safely into the driveway. Brielle feared that one day their luck would run out.

She lugged her overstuffed suitcase down the stairs to the kitchen, hugged her little brothers and stepped out the door. She disappeared into the trees. A drop of rain fell on her sleeve but she didn't notice. She picked up her pace, the suitcase bumping against her knee.

From the upstairs window Adele watched her daughter disappear into the woods toward Lost Squaw Creek. Things would work out or they wouldn't. She looked at the darkening sky then stood back from the window and let the curtain drop.

CHAPTER 5

THE GATHERING STORM

Duane Calhoun slowed as he neared the roadhouse. He checked his watch. He had plenty of time to kill before last call. Until he saw the horse trailers in the lot, he'd forgotten about Rodeo Week. Hee-haw! What a bunch of Okies.

Red had kept everything when he left, even the car she gave him but, cleverly kept in her name. She was a greedy tight-fisted woman. He'd left town in his powder blue leisure suit and the suitcase he'd come with. He deserved a lot more than he got and the injustice rankled him to the core.

A totem pole stood beside the entrance, a new addition since he'd been the mover and shaker around the joint. The caribou antlers were still tacked above the entrance, the green 1950's beer sign flickering in the window.

Duane pulled behind the building and parked in the pines above the slope that ran down to the river. Bats shot through black clouds of mosquitos. He turned off the car and listened to the tick of the over-heated engine. He kept a jug of water in the trunk, but it was too soon to take off the radiator cap without getting a face full of steam.

He lit a clove cigarette. The doc told him they could leave holes in his lungs the size of walnuts, but since his liver was shot to hell what difference did it make?

From inside the bar came the click of billiard balls and the slap of leather dice cups hitting the bar. Freddie Fender's voice spun from the juke box: *Roses are red, my love, violets are blue-ooo-ooo.* He was still a favorite after all these years. He missed the laughter and camaraderie, the free drinks and cigarettes, a little dip in the till now and then. Life was good until Red snooped into that old Margie Downs affair.

He checked the Saturday night special he kept in the glove box. It was a piece of junk he'd bought off the street when he was too high to notice the crooked site and loose barrel, but it would do close in. It came loaded so he wouldn't have to buy ammo under the watchful eye of a surveillance camera. You couldn't belch these days without being memorialized on film.

Duane looked up at the dark bedroom window above the bar. Red's kid used to sleep there. She had an unusual name he could no longer remember. If people had known what he got away with back then, he'd still be behind bars. He didn't worry about it anymore. Recovered memory tales weren't that hard to debunk.

He took a hard pull from a flask of whiskey. It burned like fire, but that didn't keep him from drinking the bottle another two fingers down. His limbs flooded with comforting warmth. He leaned back against the seat, closed his eyes and waited for closing time.

* * * *

Dyce asked Coby again. "Why didn't you pull over?"

Coby didn't like his attitude but he knew that Dyce was going through a hard transition. He had Brielle and Dyce's only companion was a ten year old roping horse.

"Like I said, I'm meeting someone. I don't have time for a lengthy conversation."

"You promised me one more season on the road."

"We've already plowed that ground, Dyce. That was before Brielle. I have to think of Grandma too. She's not half so well as she was when I took off last summer. It's her memory. She forgets things."

"Must run in the family."

Coby's temper flared.

"Get over it!" he said. "I have my own life to think about. You need to move on with yours or you'll be stuck in the same spot when you're sixty years old."

The horses sensed the tension in the air. Gunpowder shifted his weight in the horse trailer. He snorted nervously and Chili whinnied in reply.

The sky darkened. Frogs were in full chorus. The temperature dropped and Coby didn't know what else there was to say.

A banged-up green truck overloaded with hay drove by. It showered the air with golden needles, black smoke billowing from the rusted exhaust pipe.

Dyce shook fragments of hay from his hat. "Let's get off the road," he said, moving down the bank into the trees above the bayou. Coby followed, his temper once again in check.

"I know you're pushed out of shape right now," said Coby, "but that doesn't mean we can't part friends."

"With you here and me on the road all summer?" said Dyce. "I don't call that much of a friendship."

"We can meet at Gladys's at the end of the season, slam back a few cold ones, but now I've got to get on with things." Coby held out his hand as a parting gesture.

Dyce ignored him and Coby, dumbfounded, let his hand fall to his side.

"I don't know what you want from me. I really don't."

"Didn't I show you the ropes?" Dyce's voice had always been full of grit and gravel. Now there was a wounded undertone that put Coby ill at ease. He'd never seen Dyce act like this before. "Do you think you could have done as well as you did without me?"

"No. I couldn't have. Is that what you want to hear, that you made me what I am today?" He huffed a laugh. "Well, I guess you're right. I was green as grass. What you didn't tell me was how many strings were attached to our friendship. If it's money you need—"

Dyce exploded: "You don't understand. It's not about money!

"Then shut up. This conversation is over."

The frogs went quiet. Dogs barked from somewhere behind the trees.

Dyce reduced his volume a click or two. "Sorry. I didn't mean to get loud." He took a step closer, but Coby instinctively took a step back. A pine cone rolled beneath his foot. He kicked it aside and backed up another step or two."

Dyce reached out and touched Coby's shoulder.

"Don't walk away from me."

"You need to go," said Coby.

"I'm just saying, we made a good team, didn't we?"

"Yes. We made a good team."

Coby tried to shrug his hand away, but Dyce had taken hold of his jeans jacket.

"Listen kid, your parents are gone and so are mine. We lost them before we were ready to be on our own."

"That was a long time ago. I'm over it."

"No one is ever over it. Not really. It created a common bond."

Coby backed farther into the trees. Dyce's grip tightened. A metal button popped off the front of his jacket. He tried jerking free but Dyce had the strong hands of a man who'd roped and wrestled steers most of his life.

"Just answer me this, then I'll go. Didn't I treat you like a son?"

"Yeah, well maybe it was something more than that."

Another button flew into the dirt but Dyce didn't seem to notice.

Coby jerked back and hammered the bigger man's forearm with a fist, breaking his grip. In one spontaneous swing, Dyce landed a blow squarely on Coby's jaw, a punch the young man didn't see coming, a punch that surprised Dyce as much as it surprised Coby.

The snap of cartilage was audible. A tooth shot into the cat tails along the bayou. Coby flew backward, hitting his head on the trunk of a pine tree with astonishing force. He slumped to the ground, chin on chest, one leg twisted awkwardly beneath him, his hat rolling away to the side. Dyce waited, his face flushed with emotion. He expected the younger, quicker Coby to get up and knock him to kingdom come, but the kid didn't move.

Dyce bunted his thigh with the toe of his boot.

"Get up," he said. "Get up, damn you!"

Coby didn't move.

There was no response.

The evening was suddenly very still.

Dyce's anger left as quickly as it had come. He knelt beside the crumpled figure of his friend. Twisted on the ground Coby looked like a boy who'd fallen from the branch of an apple tree.

"Coby, get up! Stop clowning around."

He patted the kid's face but he was pale and unresponsive. Blood ran from his nose and trickled from the corner of his mouth. Dyce straightened his leg. He searched for the carotid artery and felt a pulse. Thank god! A pulse.

"Come on, partner. I didn't mean it. I didn't mean any of it." *I'm just a lonely selfish, jerk.*

He dropped to his knees and pulled Coby against his chest. His head lolled against Dyce's shoulder like a puppet with broken strings. After a few minutes he leaned Coby back against the tree. He put the hat back on his head and buttoned his jacket—except of course, where the buttons were missing. He felt terrible. He'd order him another jacket, a good one from Cabela's catalogue.

There was a rattling in the distance. Dyce stood up, the knees of his jeans dirty and damp. It was cold and windy but sweat ran from his hairline down his forehead.

The rain came down more steadily now, windblown drops tapping his hat and washing the dust from the toes of his boots. From a mile distant the green truck was coming back, moving faster now. The last dim light faded to darkness.

Dyce didn't want to be seen by anyone, especially Brielle if she was meeting Coby here. He couldn't make sense of what had happened just now. He'd never hit anyone except in self-defense and Coby was the last person in the world he wanted to hurt.

Dyce scrambled up the bank and started his engine thinking the rain would likely bring Coby around. He was a tough kid. He'd taken harder hits in the arena. Brielle would find him. He'd be okay.

Dyce fired up the truck, swung around Coby's horse trailer and rolled over the bridge. As he passed the hay truck all he saw was a shadowy figure behind the wheel. He hoped that was all the driver had seen of himself.

The wind whipped up and rain blew like silver beads past the headlights. He was miles down the road before he felt he could breathe again.

CHAPTER 6

LOST

Dressed in stone-washed jeans and a cable knit sweater, Brielle trotted along the path, her suitcase growing heavier with each step. The sky was dark and threatening. The wind whipped up and the rain came down, lightly at first, then in cold buckets. If she knew the rains were coming this early she'd have grabbed a raincoat on her way out the door but it was too late to turn back and still get to the bridge on time.

There was a blinding flash. Brielle dropped to her knees and covered her head. Lightning had struck a tree twenty feet off the path leaving her ears ringing. Smoke rose in a cloud from the shattered stump and floated into the trees like a ghost. Pete had told her that trees attract lightning. It could rip skin from bone and turn bone to ash. She grabbed her suitcase and moved on. She would be safe when she got to Coby's truck.

Wind snatched at her umbrella. A metal spoke snapped, then two. She clung to the handle with both hands, dropping the suitcase and flashlight. One side of the umbrella collapsed. Rain flattened her hair and soaked her running shoes. A tornado siren went off in the distance. Tornado Alley. That's what they called this part of the state.

She stopped to catch her breath and push the wet hair from her eyes. When she reached for her suitcase and flashlight, the wind wrenched the umbrella from her hand, settling it on a high branch where it flapped like a giant bat. She pushed on, not certain she was on the right path.

By now Coby would be at the bridge. Would he wait or think she wasn't coming? If he looked for her it wouldn't be in woods, but along the road. She walked briskly for another ten minutes.

A pack of growling, snapping redbone hounds flung themselves against a wire fence to the right of the path. The rusty metal squealed like a tone-deaf kid torturing a violin. She'd missed the cut-off and found herself at the back of the Rivette's property. The dogs yelped and tumbled backward as they reached the outer limit of their shock collars. Hand-scrawled signs in French were nailed to the fence posts. *Keep Out. Survivors Will Be Shot.*

The Rivette's were like their dogs, threatening and dangerous. Brielle backtracked, searching for the detour to the bridge. The darkness deepened. Half an hour was lost.

She turned in a circle, trying to get her bearings but nothing in the black and grey shadow-world looked familiar. She clung to one comforting thought. When she found her way, Coby would be waiting at the bridge.

Brielle wasn't usually superstitious, but the tales brought here from the Old Country seemed suddenly real. She imagined the *loup garou* leaping from the darkness and sinking his wolf- teeth into her throat.

A vine encircled her foot. Her ankle twisted and she hit the ground with a sharp yelp, her flashlight striking a tree, the bulb going out with a pop. Her clothes were soaked, her sweater snagged and muddy, her foot unable to bear her weight. She freed herself from the vine, sat on her suitcase and cried into her hands.

* * * *

The worst of the storm caught up with Dyce in the rolling plains fifty miles down the road from the bridge. Lightning hit a metal fence post alongside the road and danced down the barbwire like the devil on a string. He slowed when a strong blast of wind rocked the horse trailer.

No matter how far Dyce went or how fast, he couldn't shake the image of Coby's head hitting the tree trunk like a motorcycle helmet impacting pavement.

He'd only wanted to talk. He never intended for things to get out of hand. The French girl had ruined everything and he'd simply wanted to turn the tide back in his favor. It was that and more, feelings that hung in the air, unarticulated and undefined.

He kept seeing Coby slide to the ground with one leg crumpled beneath him.

He pulled into an empty rest stop in the middle of nowhere and turned back in the direction of Lost Squaw Creek. He drove against the wind, smoking through his dwindling supply of cigarettes, finishing a roll of antacids, the truck guzzling gas he couldn't afford to burn. The temperature plummeted. The rain turned to bullets. He drove through small towns that no one except the residents had heard of, each one with a country store anchored by a couple old-fashioned gas pumps.

He saw an Amish barn with a hex near the peak of the roof. From the farmhouse a lamp glowed behind a blue curtain, a sign that a young girl of marriageable age was open to receiving like-minded suitors.

For Dyce, that like-minded person had never appeared. As a relationship began to look promising he'd find some way to screw it up for reasons he couldn't fathom. No matter how sweet, no matter how beautiful, she was never *the one*.

The heater stopped working and the windows fogged. He thumped the dash and the heater whirred back to life. He wiped the windshield with his leather-gloved hand and turned the wipers up a notch.

There were softer places to live than the northern plains, places where roses bloomed in December and tanned bodies sprawled like cats on sandy beaches, places where farmers didn't die in tractor rolls and drivers didn't slide over black ice into lakes and the grills of 18 wheelers. On the other hand there was nothing more beautiful than the gold and scarlet trees of October or the first snowfall even when you knew the bitter cold would follow.

Ten years ago he'd stopped in Abundance on route to a hunting lodge. It seemed like there was a deer in the back of every pickup truck or strapped to the bumper of every car. Until that moment he couldn't figure out what to do with the money he'd saved over the years. The place felt right, so he bought a fifty acre spread outside of town. When his rodeo years were over, he'd have a place to hang his hat and not a damn soul to share it with.

By the time Dyce rumbled over the Lost Squaw, his stomach was in a knot. Sparks of ice shot past the windshield. He drove over the bridge and parked on the side of the road. Coby's truck and horse trailer were gone. He felt a guarded sense of relief. He and Brielle were probably settled in for the night at his grandmother's house. Maybe things weren't as bad as he'd imagined.

Dyce threw a slicker over his head, grabbed a flashlight and trotted across the road. He half walked, half slid down the bank and shined his light on the base of the tree where Coby had fallen. He was gone. He had to be. His vehicle wasn't here. To reassure himself, he swept the surrounding area with the light but saw nothing but the eyes of frogs glowing like jewels along the bank. He widened his search until he was convinced that Coby had left.

Dyce scrambled back up the bank and took one last look around. Rain had washed away every footprint and tire track. There was nothing to suggest that anyone had been here. As soon as he was gone, all evidence of his return would be washed away too. He remembered the truck with the hay, but decided not to obsess on it.

Somewhere back in the trees came the same deep-throated barking he'd heard earlier in the evening. He didn't know if the dogs were tethered or free but they sounded big and mean. He was headed across the road to the truck when he heard a plaintive sound coming from a different location deep in the woods. It was much like the sound of a small animal set upon by predators. As he listened more closely the sound blew away in the wind and the dogs went silent.

Back at the truck Dyce fired up a cigarette. The hail had softened to slush. He watched it stream down the windshield like silver tears. By the time the cigarette burned his fingers he'd decided more needed to be done.

What if Coby hadn't *walked* away? What if he'd been carried out, unconscious or—worse? Chili could be with Animal Control and his truck and trailer in the lot at the sheriff's substation. Had he hooked up with Brielle? Had he staggered to the road and been transported to the hospital by a passing motorist? But, if that were true, his truck would still be here.

Dyce drove toward Abundance. The substation was dark with two patrol cars in the otherwise empty lot. He continued through the comatose town and out to the Dillon place. He coasted quietly to a stop across from the house and let the engine idle. The windows were dark. The scene was silent except for rain rushing through the downspouts. There was no evidence of Coby or his truck.

Dyce pulled an address book from the glove compartment and looked up the number of the nearest hospital. The charge on his cell was low but he got a weak signal and tapped in the number.

"Community Hospital. How may I help you?"

"I'd like to speak with Coby Dillon," he said. "He was admitted earlier this evening."

"Sorry, we don't buzz the rooms after ten."

"How about a room number?"

A few seconds passed.

"I'm checking, sir. No one is registered under that name."

"Try Jacob. Coby is a nickname."

"I'm sorry. There's no Jacob either."

"Thank you." Dyce clicked off. He felt a surge of relief. Coby and Brielle had probably gone to the city to spend their first night in a nice hotel. His shoulders relaxed. He was making far too much of this. He shifted into gear and got back on the road.

CHAPTER 7

DEADLY INTENTIONS

Gladys dimmed the lights to signal last call and customers filed out the door, laughing and splashing across the parking lot to their vehicles. Rain battered the plate glass window that looked across the highway into a dark field of drenched corn.

The ditches along the roadways flowed with run-off as Wheezy McGee finished loading the beer mugs in the dishwasher. Wheeze, now in his seventies, had been an up-and-coming featherweight contender in a previous incarnation. When he won a fight he was supposed to throw, three Detroit cops on the outfit's payroll cornered him in an alley and crushed every bone in his right hand. They cut his throat to within a whisper of his jugular vein and left him for dead.

When he got out of the hospital, with nothing but his integrity intact, he left Detroit for his native Wisconsin. He never fought again and never looked back. With his career down the tubes, he climbed in the bottle and pulled the cork in behind him.

He'd been a regular at Gladys's for years before she hired him as her second in command. Now he waits bar and sleeps in an upstairs bedroom where Gladys stores cases of Guinness and broken bar stools. He feels more at home here than any place he's ever lived.

Gladys slipped a one hundred dollar bill in Wheezy's shirt pocket. Rodeo week had been one hell of a ride.

"A little extra something to blow at the Hochunk Casino," she said.

He smiled at Gladys. "You're a good old gal."

Gladys wore her signature outfit: black leather jeans, black tank top with a Harley-Davison logo and silver skull earrings. At 50-something she looked about 65 with her dyed red hair and a complexion pickled and smoked from decades of alcohol and tobacco use. That didn't mean that a certain kind of man—like the four she'd married and divorced—didn't find her husky voice and precancerous cough irresistibly sexy. Despite her excesses she'd maintained a trim figure with sculpted arms that hoisted cases of whiskey like a stevedore.

"Want me to lock up?" said Wheezy.

Gladys looked up from tallying the bank deposit.

"You go on up." she said. "When I finish here I'm going out front for some fresh air and a cigarette."

Wheezy went up the narrow staircase to his room. He moved across the floor by the faint green glow of the exit light at the back of the building. Rain shadows rippled down the wallpaper, its abstract pattern of circles and squares softly antiqued with nicotine. His favorite time was when the bar emptied out and he could enjoy the quiet seclusion of his room and a good paperback book.

He put his hundred dollar bill under the base of the bedside lamp and jingled his tips into an empty fish bowl. Gladys's biggest profits of the year were made on Rodeo Week. She wasn't much of a spender and Wheezy often wondered what she did with all that cash. Standing at the rear window he looked out at the rain puddling in the empty parking lot.

On the far side of town lightning danced on golden spider legs around the bubble-top water tower and below the pine grove the swollen waters of the Little Papoose thundered over the rocks. Wheezy was done in. All he wanted to do was to soak his bunions and read himself to sleep.

He was about to snap on the bedside lamp when he saw the shadowy outline of a car parked in the trees above the empty parking lot. The ruby cinder of a cigarette glowed behind the car windshield. He watched, unobserved, from the dark windowpane.

Instead of leaving, the driver stepped into the rain, his shoulders hunched, his hat pulled low on his forehead, a grey on grey shadow ghosting through the rain. He flicked his cigarette butt to the ground and pulled up the collar of his coat as he walked toward the bar. For a brief moment his image was caught in the green glow. Wheeze couldn't see much beyond a jailhouse swagger, but that was enough to put him on notice.

The man walked down the side of the building toward the entrance. Wheezy hustled down the inner staircase to get Gladys inside before the stranger reached her.

The bank pouch sat on the counter and he shoved it beneath the bottles and cans in the waste basket as he went by. He was half way to the door when Gladys stumbled into the room, a gun pressed against her spine.

Wheezy backed up, hands above his head.

"What have we here, Old Father Time?" laughed the man with the gun.

"Let him be," said Gladys.

Wheezy and Gladys stood still for a pat-down. The man pulled a cell phone from Gladys's pocket and struck it against the hard edge of the nearest table top. It shattered into several pieces, the battery smacking the gunman near his eye. Gladys failed to keep a straight face and paid for it with an uninspired whack to the head. There was a vague familiarity about him but nothing she could put her finger on. Beneath the whiskey on his breath was the odor of illness. She turned her head away.

He pressed the gun to her temple, keeping his chin down and his hat pulled low. He prodded them both toward the bar. As they passed the hall leading to the restrooms the pay phone caught his eye. He tried pulling it off the wall but only managed to loosen it an inch or two from the paneling before letting out a groan and clutching his side. The stranger was clearly not up to phone-wrenching, but his failure made him more aggressive.

"Open the register," he said.

The gunman didn't know it was empty and Gladys didn't know what had become of the bank pouch. Her hope lay in the Derringer hidden beneath the cash drawer.

The old boxer was reading the stranger's body-talk, how he listed to one side when he walked, how he favored that tender spot beneath his right rib-cage. Like every boxer, Wheezy knew the position of every internal organ in the human body. He also knew how to punish each one to devastating effect. His trainer once said: *A lion conserves energy. He waits for the animal with the limp.* Wheezy was looking at that animal.

The stranger waved his gun at Gladys. "Speed it up."

Did that tinny piece of junk qualify as a gun? As far as Gladys was concerned it was a Cracker Jack prize. Nevertheless, at close range it could kill her as dead as a bazooka. If she was lucky it would blow up in his face.

"Get me a Bud Lite while she decides if she wants die for a couple nickels and dimes," he said.

While Wheezy set a cold Bud in front of him, Gladys slipped the key out from under the register. She noticed the can of bear spray wasn't sitting on the counter to her right. She glanced at Wheezy but he played a dead hand.

The gunman downed his beer in a single breath, then patted the inside breast pocket of his trench coat. His hand shook as he produced a pack of smokes and pulled one out with his teeth to keep his gun hand free. He returned the pack to his pocket and fumbled out a book of matches. Once lighted, he filled his lungs with smoke and coughed it back out with a light spray of blood.

"Take thirty more seconds and I'll shoot you where you stand," he said, between a few ragged coughs.

"The key's bent," said Gladys. "It takes a second." It turned on the third try.

"Come on, come on! I don't have all night," he said, waving the gun.

She wanted to ask him if he was late for a hot date, but to her credit, she kept her mouth shut for once.

The register was a scrolled metal antique she treasured. It opened a crack. If it went wider he'd see there was nothing in the drawer. She had to get to the gun beneath it.

The man smoked his cigarette half way down, the scent of burning clove filling the air. Gladys felt dizzy. Her stomach lurched. The smell combined with the raspy voice fleshed out a person from her past—number four—Duane Lester Calhoun. She spun around and looked hard at the shadowy face beneath the hat.

"Duane! My god, what are you doing here?"

"Hi Red. Miss me?"

His mouth twisted into a lopsided grin and she nearly passed out.

"What are you doing here?"

"You already said that. Looks like I'm cleaning you out—sweetheart. No time like the present to cough up some of those marital assets."

"That was a long time ago," she said.

She was tempted to mention they'd never been legally married and that he'd probably killed Margie Downs. She held her tongue.

"Not as far back as my memory goes," he said.

The whites of his eyes were yellow like his cigarette-stained teeth. His skin was dull and slack. He'd lost at least 40 lbs. since she'd seen him last. If she'd passed him on the street she wouldn't have recognized him, the guy she'd once loved—or at least lusted for.

"I bet you thought I was still in lockup. Can you believe they let me out on good behavior?"

"I had no idea where you were," she said.

"I've been thinking that we should take that honeymoon we always talked about. Niagara Falls, wasn't it?"

"I'm not going anywhere with you," she said.

In one swift movement she jerked the cash drawer free of the register and flung it at his head. He ducked as she grabbed her Derringer, adrenaline shooting through her limbs. Duane knocked her arm aside, grabbed her by the hair on both sides of the head and slammed her face full force into the bar. She hit with a sound like a bag of ice falling to the sidewalk from a great height, then slid silently to the floor, her gun spitting a bullet harmlessly into the ceiling.

Wheezy reached beneath the bar and came up with the can of bear spray. He blasted Duane in the eyes from a foot away. The gun fell from his hand and skittered across the floor, the cigarette dropping from his mouth. He roared, his eyes clamped shut against the chemical burn. He swung his arms wildly, knocking the can against a row of bottles behind the bar. Duane forced his eyes open a crack with his fingers. It was like viewing a black and grey world from under six feet of water.

He bent over and swept his hand across the floor, feeling for his gun. Wheezy found his opening and delivered a powerful blow to the right side of Duane's back. Duane let out a roar and stumbling forward, kicked the gun beyond reach. The barrel bounced free and rolled across the floor like the wheel of a toy car.

Wheezy went for Gladys's Derringer, but by the time he retrieved it from her limp fingers, Duane was staggering out the door. Wheezy aimed and pulled the trigger. The bullet missed Duane's ear by an inch. It all happened so fast, Wheezy couldn't tell if it was a hit or a miss. As Duane fled into the night Wheezy locked and bolted the door. He grabbed change from the kitty on the bar and dinged a few coins into the pay phone.

CHAPTER 8

A LIGHT IN THE WOODS

Something warm and wet slid across Brielle's cheek. Her eyes blinked open to rain and total darkness. She felt a sharp moment of panic that brought her fully into the moment. She swiped at her cheek and felt damp fur and floppy ears. Bloodhound ears. A warm breath buffeted her skin—a sharp yip—a whine.

"Watson," she said, breaking into tears and wrapping her arms around the wet dog.

Watson was Charlie's dog from Thistle Hill on the other side of Lost Squaw Creek. He pawed her shoulder and nudged her arm. *Get up, Brielle!* She tried, but couldn't. Her ankle was too painful to support her weight.

A flashlight sliced through the trees. A man's voice called her name.

"Over here," she called. "Over here, Charlie!"

There was the snap and crackle of foliage and a shower of water sluiced from the leaves. The light came closer and suddenly Charlie was kneeling beside her. He ran the flashlight from the top of her head to her swollen ankle.

"Charlie, I'm freezing. I twisted my ankle. I can't get up."

He removed his mackintosh and wrapped it around her shoulders.

"Give me your hands," he said. She raised her arms and he pulled her upward until she stood on one quivering leg. "Okay, up we go," he said, lifting her into his arms with her head resting against his shoulder. "The suitcase can wait until morning."

With Brielle securely in his grasp, he moved sure-footedly through the rugged terrain.

In twenty minutes she was sitting in the warmth of Charlie's car, she and Watson towel dried, the dog lying on his blanket in the back seat.

Charlie poured her a cup of hot chocolate from his thermos. By the time she finished it her teeth had stopped chattering.

"Doing better?" he said.

"Much better. Thank you, Charlie." It was painful to speak. She'd called for help until her throat was raw "What time is it?"

"After two."

"Did you see anyone when you crossed the bridge?"

"The storm has driven everyone off the roads," he said.

No white truck. No Coby. Had he come for her? Looked for her? Or had he partnered up with Dyce Jackson for one more season?

She studied Charlie's face. She couldn't tell from his neutral expression what he was thinking or what his feelings were about her relationship with an outsider. Just about everyone in the family, whether they voiced it or not, was against her.

"How did you know I was here?" she asked. "I was supposed to be gone hours ago."

"Watson kept going to the door, walking in circles. He was trying to tell me something and I finally followed him. When we got to the woods, he found you."

"I called for help until I lost my voice. He must have heard me. The rain would have washed away my scent."

"Let's get you home. You need to get out of those wet clothes"

"No, Charlie, please! I can't face Mom and Pete looking like the mouse the cat dragged in. I'm supposed to be gone and I don't know what to tell them. I need time to think things through."

"You're right. You can come to my place. No sense waking up the family. Things will look better in the morning."

Brielle wasn't so sure.

They drove to the top of Thistle Hill. When they pulled up to the house a car was parked by the garage and a girl was looking under a flower pot on the porch. She wore a red fox jacket, thigh high boots and a leather mini-skirt that provided minimum coverage. The blonde hair piled on top of her head was straggling out of its pins.

Brielle glanced at Charlie. He tightened the muscles in his jaw.

"Wait here. This will only take a minute," he said.

He exited the car.

The rain had subsided, at least for the moment. When Brielle rolled her window down a few inches fragments of conversation drifted her way.

She heard the girl say *key.*

"I don't leave it out anymore," said Charlie.

"Sorry it's so late, but the bar just closed and I didn't want to leave before my friends did." Charlie did not respond. "Aren't you going to say something?"

"This isn't a good time."

"I'm freezing out here."

"You need to go home, Suzette."

Suzette? Brielle hadn't recognized her own cousin. She didn't look anything like she had at church on Sunday.

"Why? I just got here. We have all night."

"I don't think so."

"Where have you been? I've been waiting for almost an hour."

"There was a family emergency."

"An emergency? I hope Adele put a slug in Old Lady Revette," she said, wobbling on her skyscraper high heels.

The wind whipped up and some of the words went with it.

"If she doesn't stop—the old bat—end up at the bottom of Granite Drop."

If who doesn't stop what? Granite Drop is the suicide jump, but not everyone takes the dive voluntarily.

Suzette looked toward Charlie's car and saw Brielle dimly illuminated in the light from the dash. The wind reversed direction and settled down.

"Oh god, tell me that isn't the Broussard's little virgin princess," said Suzette. "What happened to her cowboy? I thought they were riding into the sunset tonight."

"You've had too much to drink. We can talk another time."

"She's pretty enough for a Broussard, I guess, but I bet she won't do this for you," she said, pressing her body against Charlie's and kissing him on the mouth. He neither resisted nor reacted. She laughed and stepped back, then ripped open the front of her jacket with a flourish. There was nothing under it, at least in the line of clothing. "Just so you know what you're missing," she said, with a toss of her head.

Suzette spun around, went down the porch steps. She wobbled toward the passenger side of Charlie's car. Watson growled deep in his throat. Brielle rolled the window half way down.

"Hello, Suzette," she said, in a neutral tone.

"Well, aren't you a mess."

"I suppose I am. I got turned around in the woods."

Suzette reached inside the car and grabbed the front of the mackintosh getting a few strands of Brielle's hair twisted around her ring. Brielle winced.

"You'll stay away from Charlie if you know what's good for you," she said.

Brielle jerked free, a few hairs ripping off on Suzette's ring.

Charlie came up behind her and dragged Miss Fox Jacket to her car. He opened the door, pushed her inside and slammed it shut.

Why did Suzette feel so threatened? Brielle was in love with Coby. There was no room in her life for two men, although she bet that Suzette could find room for three or four.

She watched with relief as Suzette drove down the hill and Charlie walked back to the car.

"You okay?" he said. "Your cousin is in one of her moods."

"I'm fine.

"She's usually only half this drunk."

Brielle laughed and Charlie smiled. He helped her out of the car and Watson followed.

"I can walk a little now if I'm careful," she said. "I think I twisted it more than sprained it."

"There you go. Lean on my arm."

"Thank you for finding me."

"I'll have to share that honor with Watson," he said. "Come inside. I'll throw some logs on the fire."

As she limped to the house she thought about what her little brother Anton had said. *Suzette Rochon is hot to trot.* Her temper was pretty hot too.

CHAPTER 9

A PORTRAIT IN BLOOD

The ringing of the bedside phone wakes me. Frack stirs. The digital clock reads 2:45 A.M. The caller I.D. reads Gladys's Bar. That would be the pay phone. Gladys's cell phone reads Gladys Calhoun.

I press talk and put the call on speaker. Frack rises on an elbow and rolls toward me.

"Gladys?" I say.

"Robely, it's Wheeze. We've been attacked. Gladys is busted up real bad. The Emergency Medical Team is on their way."

"Where's the perp?"

"Gone."

Frack is out of bed pulling on his clothes.

"We'll be right there," I say.

As I'm getting dressed, I call Big Mike who says he'll call Sheriff Brooker and Medical Examiner, Paula Dennison.

Frack and I race through the deserted streets, siren blaring, lights flashing. We fly across the Little Papoose and skid to a stop in front of the bar. I hear the wailing in the distance as the first responders pull out of the firehouse.

Wheezy unlocks the door as soon as he hears my voice. I see a delicate bone poking through the top of his hand. Gladys's Derringer is dangling from his index finger. I gingerly take possession of the gun, set it on the table, help him to a chair.

"She's over here," calls Frack, from behind the bar.

Gladys is lying face down on the floor, fragments of broken teeth floating in a pool of blood beneath her head. I kneel next to her and hear a faint gurgling. She's breathing. I've never seen Gladys helpless like this. I'm shaken, but manage to maintain focus.

"Her pulse is faint and thready," says Frack, his fingers pressing her wrist.

"Mom! Can you hear me?"

There's no response, just red bubbles on her lips, a widening circle of red and the metallic smell of blood.

I run my hands gently over her scalp. I expect to find a bullet wound. Either there is none or I can't find it. I ask Wheezy if she's been shot. He says no, that her face was slammed into the bar. The image makes me light-headed.

I see her broken nose and shattered face, a frightening amount of arterial blood still pulsing from her nostrils. Her face is swelling beyond recognition. I want to believe it's not her, but there's her Harley-Davidson t-shirt, silver skull earrings and red hair.

Frack is kneeling beside me.

"You okay?" he says.

I nod.

If someone had asked me ten years ago, or even ten days ago, if I loved Gladys, I'd have had to think twice. She was a distant, self-centered, seldom-sober mother, but at this moment I know I don't want her energy leaving this planet—not this soon—not this way.

The EMTs push through the door with their medical arsenal. I tell them how Gladys sustained her injuries, then back off and let them do their job.

Pieces of a second gun are scattered across the floor. I circle them with chalk and leave them in situ. Collection of evidence is the job of the M.E. and her forensics team.

Wheezy looks so small and helpless sitting there alone. I get a blanket from upstairs and throw it around his thin shoulders. I bring him a bottle of apricot brandy and a glass. He puts the bottle to his lips and drinks it half way down. We sit with him while the medics work on Gladys.

"Did you recognize the person who did this?" I ask. "Was there more than one?"

"Just the one guy. He got the drop on us just as we were closing.

"Have you seen him before?"

"No, but Gladys has. She called him Duane."

After a second of stunned silence, I say: "Duane Calhoun!"

"I imagine so."

The name goes way back, but not far enough that it doesn't drudge up a lot of negative vibes.

I turn to Frack. "He was Gladys's fourth husband, Duane Lester Calhoun. He hasn't been around for years, ever since I was a kid."

Wheezy gives a description. Frack gets on his Smart Phone and sends out a BOLO—Be On The Lookout, although we have no idea if he's nearby or in the wind.

"Duane said Gladys cheated him out of his marital assets," says Wheezy, reciting a blow by blow of the night's events. "Duane wanted money but Gladys had already prepared the bank deposit and there was nothing in the till. As soon as I saw him coming toward the building I knew he was trouble. He waited until everyone else was gone. I hid the deposit under some empties in the basket behind the bar. He got nothing from me but a face full of bear spray."

"That was a smart move," says Frack. "We'll put the money in the safe at the station for now. Do you realize a bone is sticking through the top of your hand?"

"I do. The pain is just starting to kick in," he says. "Feels like I've been bit by a rattlesnake."

"We'll get you taken care of. I promise."

"Calhoun is sick. He looked like a dead man walking," says Wheezy. "The whites of his eyes were yellow. He turned gray and almost collapsed when I punched him in the liver."

"Did you get a bullet off?"

"I don't know. You'd think I'd remember something like that. Gladys popped one into the ceiling when she collapsed, so if the chamber's empty I got one off. Those muff guns only hold two bullets."

Big Mike Oxenburg, strides through the door with a high-powered flashlight in his hand and a big non-regulation six-shooter on his hip that had once belonged to his grandfather.

"Duane's car is back in the trees," says Wheezy. "I heard his keys drop so he won't be driving out of here."

I tell Mike what I know and he leaves to check the perimeter of the building and the bank above the river. An ambulance pulls in and Gladys, still unconscious, is loaded onto a stretcher. As she passes through the room I squeeze her hand. It's cold and unresponsive. She's wearing an oxygen mask and a tube is dripping clear fluid into a vein. "Is she—?" I begin.

"She's still with us. We're taking her to General. You coming?"

"I can't. I have to wait for the M.E." I give him my cell phone number. "Have the doctor call me. Mr. McGee has to go too. His hand is in bad shape."

Within moments both wounded warriors are on their way to the E.R.

After twenty minutes Mike reenters the bar. He's winded, his slicker dripping rain. "Even with the flashlight it's hard to get around back there."

I see a set of car keys on the floor.

"If those are the perp's he'll be on foot. We're looking for a man named Duane Lester Calhoun. You may have heard the name before."

"*That* Calhoun?"

"Yup. He's one of a kind. Unlucky Number Four," I say. "He may have hitched a ride or commandeered a car but at this time of night, I doubt it." I check the Derringer as we speak. "Wheeze got a shot off, but we don't know if Calhoun was hit. He did however deliver a face full of bear spray and a fist to a possibly ailing liver. My guess is Calhoun's hiding somewhere between the river and this side of the highway. He might have gone across the road into the corn field, but I doubt it."

"Listen Robely, I've done what I can tonight," says Mike. "In the morning I'll assemble a search party. The rain has probably washed away any scent but the dogs are still good at sighting their target. I'll call Jim's Towing and have the car moved to the lot so we can go over it in the morning. It might give us an idea where he came from or who he's in contact with."

"Or who he stole it from," says Frack.

"Right. Robely, you're lead. Partner with Frack. You okay with that?"

"Sure, Boss."

"I thought Brooker and Dennison were on their way," says Mike.

"It takes Paula time to round up her team at this hour."

With the exception of one item, I leave potential evidence in place. I pick up a half-smoked cigarette beneath a bar stool that could possibly be overlooked. There's no lipstick on the filter. I'm thinking male DNA. Wheezy has already swept the floor which makes this a significant find. It has to have been dropped after closing time. As I drop it into a glycine envelope the scent hits me in a disturbing way I can't explain. Clove. That spicy, smoky smell. A memory begins to surface but I shove it into a dark box and slam down the lid.

"You look like you've seen a ghost," says Frack.

"Not important," I say.

The door opens and Sheriff Brooker arrives with Medical Examiner, Paula Dennison and her forensics team. Once the M.E. is on site, the crime scene is hers. Her authority supersedes that of the deputies, the sheriff and the President of the United States for that matter.

On a day to day basis, Paula and Brooker work hand in hand at the county morgue. She processes crime scenes, performs autopsies and submits her conclusions to Brooker in written form. The Death Certificate will contain, among other information, Cause and Manner of Death.

Brooker is our Sheriff/Coroner but coroners do not perform autopsies, at least in modern times. That's the function of the M.E. Unless the coroner feels more investigation is warranted, he signs the Death Certificate, affixes his official seal and files it with the County Clerk.

I hand her the envelope with the cigarette and explain why it could be significant. She puts it in a larger bag with the Derringer and the pieces of Duane's gun.

Paula asks Frack and me to hang around until she's through processing the scene. There's something important she wants to discuss, something other than the case at hand.

By 4:30 A.M, Paula releases the crime scene and the three of us are alone.

Frack leaves a message on the answering machine of a business in Appleton that specializes in crime scene clean up. Despite the hour they return our call and an appointment is set up for the morning.

CHAPTER 10

FRENCH MOONLIGHT

"Okay, let's have it," I say, once we're settled in a corner booth. "It's been a long night. I'm tired and I want to go home."

Paula gets to the point. "In the last few months I've autopsied three adult males. One had gone blind overnight. Another suffered early onset dementia and a third had kidney failure. They'd all presented to different doctors with different symptoms, so no obvious link was detected between the cases. I examined blood samples post mortem and discovered lethal levels of lead in all three men.

"Lead poisoning? How does that happen?" I say.

"We most often see it in children who chew windowsills or eat contaminated paint chips off old buildings. It retards brain development and leads to learning disabilities. A common source of accidental contamination in adults is during renovation or demolition of old buildings where aerosolized lead paint is inhaled."

"Are you saying all these men worked construction?" I ask.

"If that were true I would already have put these cases to bed," says Paula, "but the oldest gentleman ran a commercial fishing dock—and no—he didn't swallow a lead sinker. Subject number two, a middle-aged, healthy male until recently, picked up and delivered dead farm animals to the rendering plant. The third man was only twenty-three and confined to a wheelchair after a diving accident. How many other lead-related deaths slipped by unnoticed, we'll probably never know."

"Then it's obviously not work-related," I say. "What's the common denominator?"

"They were all alcoholics."

"I'm not following."

"Lead fittings on whiskey stills," says Frack. "It happened a lot during Prohibition."

"Correct," says Paula. "I recently picked the brain of a chemistry professor at Lawrence College. He knows everything there is to know about distilling spirits and imparted a lot of valuable information. You want to hear some of the names they come up with for the home-grown product?"

"Sure," I say.

"Skunk. Donkey Punch. Ruckus Juice. Block and Tackle and my favorite, Tiger Sweat."

"Pretty colorful. Any idea where this stuff is coming from?"

"The professor provided a clue. Down south the generic for illegal spirits is Moonshine or White Lightning. Locally he's heard it referred to as French Moonlight."

"French Moonlight. Sounds romantic, like an exotic perfume," I say.

"I'm sure it's lovely until it kills you. My focus is not on clean stills. They produce a product as pure as the Everclear you buy at the liquor store. The chemical footprint is identical, except Everclear comes with a government seal and all the fancy taxes that go with it. Who wants to pay taxes? The moonshiners don't. They see nothing wrong with sticking it to the government."

"Join the club," I say.

The three of us laugh conspiratorially.

"I assume most of the local stills are clean," continues Paula. "We'd never find them all anyway, so I want to concentrate on tracking down the one or two that are heavily contaminated. Those we need to shut down. Judging by its name, it would likely be coming from Frenchman Wood."

"I heard that part of the county has never been accurately mapped," says Frack, "at least not in minute detail. It would be like looking for a needle in a haystack and not finding the haystack."

"You're right, except for one major clue," says Paula, "The surnames of the dead men."

"How is that a clue?"

"Petit. Dubois. Bonnet. They drank from the same poison well and I want to see it run dry. The distillers aren't selling to the legit bars like Gladys's or even Bubba's, so we can scratch those off the list. If they were, we'd have figured this out long ago. The French are selling to their own people maybe through the jukes back in the woods, or word of mouth.

"The addresses of the deceased must be in their medical files," I say.

"All fictitious."

"How hard is it to set up a moonshine operation?" I ask.

"It doesn't take a fortune. You can purchase stills of varying capacities over the Internet but that would leave a paper trail. With a little know-how a moonshiner can set up his own operation. Then all he needs is corn, water, sugar, yeast and expertise."

"So where are you going to begin?" I ask.

"I was hoping to begin with you. Why do you think we're having this conversation?"

"Me? I'm not ATF? I hand out traffic tickets and break up scuffles at Bubba's. This is outside of my job description."

"ATF leaves it to local law enforcement these days. A small operation like this isn't big enough to set their antennae quivering. It's not like we're Chicago in the Roaring 20's. Come on, Robely. It doesn't hurt to do a little poking around."

"Where?"

"Where else? Frenchman Wood."

"I'd stand out like a sore thumb. No one wanders around The Wood unless they live there. And one more thing—in case you're brain dead—have you forgotten what happened to my mother and Wheezy just hours ago? I'm lead on the case. I have no time for this."

"Relax Robely. I don't mean this minute. Give yourself a week or two. It'll take your mind off Gladys. Unless you know how to use a scalpel there's nothing you can do for her anyway."

"Thanks, Paula. You're real sensitive. Ever stop to think I might want to use my time hunting down the guy who tried to kill her? Why don't *you* do something? They're your bodies."

"I only deal with the dead." She smiles sweetly. "They're less likely to fill me with buckshot."

"The people back in The Wood want to be left alone," I say.

"So did Bonnie and Clyde."

4:00 ...AM

Frack and I are finally alone in the bar. It's almost dawn and so quiet I hear the electrical buzz from the clock across the room. Soon farmers will be getting up for the first milking and fishermen will be off to their favorite fishing holes.

Frack encircles me with his arms and I lean my forehead against his chest. We're both beat. When I close my eyes I see a widening circle of blood opening like a big red umbrella. I can't get the image of Gladys's battered non-face out of my head. I can't get rid of the metallic smell of blood.

I notice the worried look on Frack's face. "Don't think I'm not up to this," I say. "It's not like I haven't seen worse at accident scenes. And now Paula dumps this French Moonlight thing in my lap."

"You'll be fine after you get some sleep. I'm certain of it."

My cell phone vibrates.

"It's the hospital," I say, pressing the talk button.

After five minutes I click off and return the phone to my pocket.

"So what's the prognosis?" asks Frack.

"Not good. Gladys is still unconscious. She's critical and unstable. They don't know if she's going to make it. The priority is stopping the arterial bleed. She has crushed bones in her face, some fragments lodged in the frontal lobe of her brain. If she survives she'll be facing several surgeries, both medical and reconstructive."

Frack shakes his head. "That's terrible news. At least she's hanging on. Any word on The Wheeze?"

"The bone is set and he has a ride home with another patient. His quick thinking may very well have saved them both."

"You want to go to the hospital?"

"I'd only be in the way. They'll notify me of any changes in her condition."

I hear a car door slam. Wheezy comes through the door with his hand wrapped in a big ball of plaster and tape.

I give him a hug.

"Glad you're home, Wheezy."

"How's Gladys doing?" he asks. "They don't tell you a damn thing in the hospital."

"We probably won't know much for a few days. You want me to get someone to stay with you?"

"No thanks. I'd rather be alone. What are we going to do about the bar?"

"We'll have to shut down for now. Order what you need from the Blue-bird. Put it on my tab. I'll arrange for delivery. Anything else you need, just call me or Frack."

"What about all that blood? I've seen my share of blood in the ring, but never like this."

"A clean-up crew is coming in the morning. All you have to do is let them in and lock up when they're gone. After that we'll take things one day at a time."

Wheezy takes the bank deposit bag from its hiding place and hands it to Frack. "Take good care of it. You know how Gladys is when it comes to money."

* * * *

I collapse on the bed. I've never been so drained. I have a vague recollection of my shoes being removed, my gun being lifted from the holster, a comforter floating down on top of me.

In the deepest recess of my mind a door opens just wide enough for an eye to peek through. I know the nightmare is on the other side trying to get in. I push back as hard as I can but I'm too exhausted to hold my ground. The door explodes inward and I spiral down a vortex of darkness.

The year is vague. I'm eight, maybe nine. I wake in the night. A draft slips under my door from the hallway. The bar has been closed for hours and Gladys is passed out in her room. I hear footsteps in the hall, someone in stocking feet. The doorknob moves. I lie motionless, afraid to breathe as one of Gladys's night visitors enters the room. It's a dark night, no moon-light shining through the window. I can't make out a face. A hand clamps over my mouth. I close my eyes tight. It's a big hand that covers my whole face. I want to cry but I can't breathe.

"You make a sound and I'll burn this place down with you in it." He whispers so close to my ear I smell the drunken heat of his breath.

After a few traumatic moments he gets up and lights a cigarette. A strange-smelling smoke spirals from the cinder. It's not regular tobacco or the dirty-socks smell of marijuana that regularly fills Gladys's room. It's something I can't place, something spicy and smoky that reminds me of baked ham.

He quietly opens the door and walks down the hall to the bathroom. I run in the opposite direction for the safety of Gladys's room. She's snoring softly. I shake her. She moans. If she doesn't wake up he'll find me here and burn the place down. I shake her again and she shrugs me away. The room smells of booze and bedroom funk and that strange-smelling smoke. A gin bottle rolls out from under the bed.

Desperate, I snap on the bedside lamp.

Gladys's face shrivels against the glare. "Go back to bed," she mumbles. "And turn that damn thing off."

"Mom! Wake up. It's me, Robely."

Mascara is smeared beneath her eyes. She opens them half way. My story spills out, the story I've been too afraid to tell until now. She listens but her expression remains flat. She tells me not to stir things up, to go back to bed.

"You mention this to anyone, I mean anyone," she says, and they'll lock you in the nuthouse and throw away the key. Little girls aren't supposed to know about these things.

I knew then that nothing would change. I was nobody, just the kid who lived above Gladys's bar, the kid everybody said would never amount to a hill of beans.

I hear the toilet flush. Footsteps go downstairs to the bar. A beer tab pops and I run back to my room before the footsteps return.

I'm trapped. My grades drop. I become an angry, distrustful child who sleeps with a chair wedged beneath the doorknob. I keep the secret. I don't want to go to the nuthouse.

CHAPTER 11

MISSING

The sun bloomed across the porcelain blue sky like a giant sunflower, the storm having blown south during the night. Brielle woke to the smell of fresh brewed coffee. She was dressed in a man's soft clean pajama top and at the foot of the bed were neatly folded clothes that had been rescued from her suitcase while she'd slept the morning away. When she climbed out from the covers, Watson jumped up and took her place on the bed.

Since she was a little girl she'd always felt safe in Charlie's house. It was the size of a roomy two bedroom cabin with knotty pine walls and exposed wooden beams. He'd milled every board and pounded every nail himself. There were never stacks of dirty dishes in the sink or piles of clothes tossed about the floor like so many of the other men in the family who expected the women to clean up after them. Muddy boots and fishing gear were left on the screened back porch overlooking the pond.

On the dresser was a framed 8 x 10 photo of Julie. Charlie never said where she came from or how they met. She was a pretty girl with light brown hair and blue eyes who looked happy even on days when she struggled with pain. She stayed inside most of the time and Brielle never got to know her well.

She reached for her clothes. She was stiff and sore from the night before, but felt surprisingly rested for all she'd been through. Dressing in jeans, a sleeveless red blouse and white tennis shoes she made a quick trip to the adjoining bathroom. Once she was sufficiently pulled together, she went to the kitchen where Charlie had placed two steaming cups of coffee on the table.

"Good morning, Charlie," she said, taking a chair.

"How did you sleep?"

"I don't remember anything except getting into a warm bath."

"That's because you fell asleep in the tub. How's your ankle this morning?"

"Much better. Thanks for retrieving my suitcase. You must have been up at dawn."

"Your clothes made it through the storm, but I'm afraid your suitcase is ruined."

"I don't care about the suitcase. She blushed remembering the packet of birth control pills Mom had slipped in with her clothes. She didn't want Charlie to think poorly of her even though the card had never been taken from its wrapper. Nothing had happened between her and Coby. Maybe it never would. She took a sip of coffee. "Thanks for getting me tucked in. I'm sorry I stole your bed."

"Why? I liked the challenge of folding my six foot two frame into a wooden-armed five foot sofa."

She went for another apology but broke into laughter instead.

"Oh, you are a heartless woman," he said.

"You should have put *me* on the couch. I was so tired I wouldn't have known the difference."

"If you're hungry I can—"

"I'm fine. I have things to do and I need your help, Charlie."

"I felt that one coming." he said, tipping back in his chair with a smile, arms crossed over his chest. He'd known Brielle all his life but it was the first time he saw her as a young woman and not a child. She reminded him of a willow tree, graceful and delicate, but strong at the core.

"Why are you looking at me like that," she said, tilting her head to the side, her long dark hair falling over her shoulder.

Because you're achingly beautiful.

"Because you're the bossiest girl I've ever known," he said. "You say jump, and I'm supposed to jump."

She looked at him with eyes the color of dark honey.

"I'm in love, Charlie, and I have no one else to turn to. Mom and Pete think I've left with Coby and I'd like to keep it that way until I get a few things straightened out. I need a ride to Dane Road." Brielle smiled her most charming smile. "You will jump, won't you Charlie?"

* * * *

Dyce Dean Jackson was doing better than he thought he would after his break with Coby, at least in his rodeo performances. He was back in the land of cactus, dust and rattlesnakes where he and his old man rode when he was a kid. He forewent the larger events and returned to the small venues along the Mexico border. He'd won several events mostly in calf roping and a few bareback bucking competitions, but when night came and everything was quiet, he still couldn't get Coby out of his head.

Lying awake in his bed roll he'd stared into a vast bowl of stars hoping for that illusive something that always seemed to be around the next corner or in the next town or down the next highway.

He wondered how Coby was doing, how things were going with him and Brielle, if his jaw was okay now, if a dentist had implanted a new tooth. The only thing that helped him sleep was drinking tequila down to the worm at the bottom of the bottle.

On a hot afternoon he followed a dust devil down an unpaved road that terminated at an adobe church in the desert. The Padre who'd buried his father in the churchyard had long since passed away. Dyce wandered through the dusty plot where stacked stones kept the coyotes from digging up the graves. He could only guess which fragments of crumbling wood on the ground had once marked his old man's grave. He took his hat off to the memory of Dyce Dean Jackson, Sr. and felt a lump rise in his throat. He searched for the right words but he'd never been a church-goer and nothing came to mind.

* * * *

The phone rings at 9:30 A.M. Frack has left. I should have been up two hours ago. The vivid fragments of last night's dream still haunt me. Calhoun had been the faceless monster of my childhood, his identity unlocked by the odor of a discarded clove cigarette. It's amazing the things a child can block out so she can make it from one day to the next.

"Hello."

"Robely, it's Vickie from the Veterinary Hospital. Did I wake you?"

"Not until I had three good hours of sleep."

"Oh, I am so sorry. Did the incident at the bar have anything to do with your mom? It was all over town by the time I got to work."

"She's pretty bad off Vickie. If she makes it, it's going to be a lengthy recovery."

"I'm so sorry, sweety. I'm going to call the ladies from church and start a prayer chain."

"Thanks, Vickie. That's very kind."

"There's a big homesick dog here who wants to go home. He's had the whole works from his boosters, to his toe nails, to his perfumed flea bath. Keep in mind he's still a bit groggy from the medication."

"I will. I'll be there as soon as I can."

I call Frack. He answers on the third ring. I hear the Little Papoose galloping over the boulders, dogs baying and men calling back and forth among the trees.

"Why didn't you wake me, Frack? If it weren't for a call from the Vet's I'd still be sleeping. Fargo is ready to go."

"Big Mike's given you the day off. We have too many hands on deck as it is."

"Okay, I'll pick up Fargo. If I can't play cop how about I make dinner tonight?"

"I'd like that. I called the hospital. Gladys is the same. They say to check back late this afternoon for an update."

I leave the house wearing my shoulder holster beneath my jacket and my badge clipped to my belt. I may not be needed at the river, but I'm not letting my day go to waste.

* * * *

Charlie took the pickup so Watson could ride in the back. Brielle sat quietly as they drove through Abundance and into the countryside beyond the river. She pointed out the Dillon property at the tag end of Dane Road. Charlie parked across from the house.

Chickens ranged free in the side yard and a rooster announced their arrival from his perch on the mailbox. There was no truck in the driveway. No horse in the corral.

"I'd better check with Miss Amity," she said, jumping to the ground. She went through the front gate and up the porch steps. An elderly woman opened to her knock. She was bent and frail with bifocals balanced at an angle on her nose.

Miss Dillon squinted. "Brielle? That is you, isn't it?"

"Yes, it's me, Grandma Dillon. I'm looking for Coby?"

"Coby?" she said, like she hadn't heard the name before.

"Your grandson, Miss Dillon. That Coby."

Amity was having one of her bad memory days, like the time it took a full minute for her to remember the first name of her late husband.

"Wouldn't he be on the road by now with that handsome partner of his? He used to be the Marlboro Man you know."

"Yes, I've heard that. If you hear from Coby, please tell him Brielle was here."

"So what did she say?" asked Charlie, when she climbed back in the truck.

"She doesn't know anything. I'd forgotten Coby was starting a new job at the hardware store today."

"Then why isn't the horse here?" said Charlie. "Where's the trailer?"

"I don't know. Let's take Meadow Road back and see if his partner is still around."

Dyce's spread was a beautiful piece of land with a half-acre pond in the middle of the pasture. There was an aluminum gate across the driveway and the truck and horse trailer were gone, just like Coby's were. Could be Miss Amity was right.

"Let's try the hardware store," says Charley

Coby's truck wasn't there either. When Brielle walked in the door, Mr. Preston was pushing a broom around the worn wooden floor.

"I'm Brielle Broussard, Mr. Preston. I'm looking for my boyfriend, Coby Dillon. He was supposed to start working for you today."

"I've been waiting for Coby for hours," he said. "If you see him tell him he's fired."

"I'm trying to tell you I can't find him. He isn't where he's supposed to be."

"No kidding. I never would have guessed."

"Did he call in to say he wasn't coming, or did he simply not show?"

"Not word one. Listen, a young lady gets mixed up with a rodeo fellow all she can expect is a roll in the hay and a view of his horse's tail as he gallops out of her life."

"In that case, Mr. Preston, I'd better keep looking. I've been cheated out of my roll in the hay and I intend to collect." She jerked the door closed as she left.

Charlie was pouring water from a thermos into Watson's bowl in the bed of the truck. He jumped to the sidewalk, opened the passenger side door and tossed the thermos behind the seat.

"He never showed," said Brielle. "He never called. I'm worried. That's not like him. Even if he's taken off with Dyce he'd have found someone to stay with his grandmother. I don't know where else to look and I dread going home. Mom will give me that *I told you so* look and the boys will make a circus of it."

"Get in the truck," he said, closing the door behind her and walking around to the driver's side. He climbed behind the wheel and started the engine.

"Let's go back to my place and think things through. If he doesn't materialize by tomorrow we'll file a Missing Person's Report. If he's still in the area someone has to have seen him."

CHAPTER 12

THE MYSTERY AT GRINDING ROCK

I pick up Fargo at the vets and pay the bill. Of course he is over-joyed to see me. A little groggy, he still jumps up with his big paws on my shoulders and a nip on the chin as reprimand for his two day abandonment.

Fargo was dumped on the side of the road a few years back, hungry and full of burrs. I knew from his warm, sad eyes that he would be my *forever dog.* He eats every meal as if it's his last, then begs, borrows or steals any food that isn't nailed down.

I give him hugs and kisses and a handful of dog treats before he plunks down on his blanket in the back seat with his Raggedy Ann doll between his paws. Since he neither hunts nor herds, dogs like Fargo are not in great demand in farm country. He's not much of a watchdog either and would probably help a burglar pack up the family silver—if, of course, we had family silver.

I drive to Gladys's Bar and check on Wheezy, leaving Fargo in the car with the windows rolled down. Flowers, notes, helium balloons and teddy bears are banked against the walls of the entryway. I read a few cards, mostly from regulars, some from people I don't know and who probably don't know Gladys. Most of the messages include Wheezy as well. Careful not to step on the flowers I go inside.

Wheezy is sitting at the bar with a cup of coffee and a paperback book. The cleaning crew has come and gone, restoring the bar to its rustic glory.

"Don't forget to order lunch," I tell him. "Call me if you need anything."

I climb the bank behind the building and see the search party scouring the woods and river bank below. Frack is conferring with the dog handlers. I see no reason to interrupt the flow of progress.

I drive to the hospital. I don't want to wait until late afternoon to get an update on Gladys. I park in the shade and ride the elevator to the third floor where a nurse walks me to the critical care unit. There's a machine beeping and tubes running from bottles of liquid into her arms and wrists. It's the first time I've seen her since she was wheeled out of the bar. Her condition is still critical and unstable.

What little I see of her face is swollen and bruised beyond recognition, her head wrapped in bandages the size of a basketball. I'm told her facial fractures are comparable to a shattered egg shell, the pieces too numerous to count, some lodged in the frontal cortex of her brain.

"Have you seen injuries like this before?" I ask the nurse.

"Only once, when a man skied headlong into a tree."

"And?"

"DOA."

"Any good news?"

"We've stopped the hemorrhaging. People have actually exsanguinated from a severed nasal artery. If you want to talk to the doctor, he'll be in later."

I thank her and she moves to the bedside of another patient.

"I'm here, Mom," I tell Gladys. "Everything is going to be—"

I can't say it. I don't know if everything is going to be okay. I wonder a bit guiltily if a gentle exit from this world to that big distillery in the sky wouldn't be more merciful. No more worries. No more pain. No psychotic exes walking out of the midnight rain.

Then again, if anyone is tough enough to get through this, it's Gladys Danner Calhoun, former juvenile delinquent and general pain in the butt. I have a fleeting impulse to hug her but it would probably set off the alarm.

Instead, I gingerly squeeze her fingers avoiding the pin cushion of needles piercing her veins. There's no response, no tension of muscle or tendon. I close my eyes and see her like she was before the attack, hoisting cases of whiskey, holding three mugs of beer in each hand without spilling a drop. I hear her lusty laughter and off-color jokes, the ever-present cigarettes smoked down to a stub that will probably kill her if this doesn't.

I lean close to her ear. "Mom, it's Robely. Never give up."

Back in the car I think about Paula's tales of Frenchman Wood, about whiskey stills and French Moonlight and three bodies lying on cold slabs. When I get to Abundance I drive straight through town and keep going.

* * * *

After a forty-five minute drive I come to an unmarked road this side of Paget Store. It's the entrance to Frenchman Wood. Two elderly men sit in rockers on the front porch. A hand painted sign in the window reads Cuisses de Grenouille.

"Crees day gron u wee," I say. "Frog legs."

How did I know that? I don't speak French nor do I understand it. The words just rolled out of me like one of those crazy women who start speaking in tongues and freaking people out.

The store disappears in my rear view mirror. The road is rutted, washed out in places, full of tree roots and potholes. Thick foliage encroaches on both sides, branches brushing against the sides of the car, until a half mile in, the road opens to the light.

I drive a mile before I see widely separated driveways, probably running back to subsistence farms cut from the forest. I'd like to record a few names in my notebook, like the ones belonging to the men Paula autopsied, but there are no mailboxes, thus no names and street numbers. Like so many rural areas, residents pick up their mail at the nearest country store. Mail trucks don't hazard these roads and neither does the snowplow in winter.

There are a few other roads too, narrow and weed-choked. Most would be logging or service roads ending at a saw mill, an abandoned summer camp or a dead end. So where are the stills? I can't march onto private property and dig around, nor would I want to. I'd rather not die with a face full of buckshot. Playing ATF was not part of my curriculum at the Academy. In The Wood there is little open rolling land for corn or large pastures, no big Amish barns with colorful hexes beneath the peaks of the roofs like we have around Abundance. Every few yards signs in English or French are nailed to fence posts and trees. Keep out. No Hunting. One sign says Poison Oak, another, Beware of Hog-Nose Vipers, a rather fearsome-looking local snake. As a child I saw a sharp-fanged viper pop a bloated frog like a balloon and swallow it whole. It's an image a child doesn't soon forget.

I pull over at a shady spot along the road. Wild berries grow along a braided wire fence and birds call back and forth from the rustling treetops. I'm a few miles down the road and I haven't seen a single person, not even a child playing or riding a bike or pony. I reach for the door handle. Fargo opens an eye. "Wanna come?" I say. He groans, puts his head on the seat and goes back to sleep. I buzz the windows down and get out of the car.

I do a few stretches to loosen my muscles and walk up the road. A twister of wind rearranges my hair and whooshes through the leafy treetops. It's beautiful back here, a private Eden of sorts. The forest hasn't been exploited for its trees in decades and it's lush with pine, oak, blackberries, flowering vines and wild crabapple trees.

I have a strange feeling of *deja vu* as I get farther from the car. I come to an incline in the road. I don't remember being here before, but I know there's a bridge on the other side of the rise. How do I know that? How am I able to say frog legs in French? I have no idea.

As I top the rise, I see the bridge fifty yards ahead, exactly as I envisioned—not the modern concrete kind constructed after World War Two—but an older wooden structure that looks like it spouted from the landscape.

Beneath the bridge flows a clear slow-moving creek. Upstream to the right is a bayou filled with waterlilies, the water so clear I can see fish darting in the shade of the cattails. The waterway is too sleepy and narrow to be a tributary of the bounding Little Papoose River, so it must be a branch of the Lost Squaw. I feel a visceral connection to this place, but can't say why.

I cross the bridge. On the other side, to the right and down a path above the creek is a large rock. I've seen that rock before. I *know* that rock. I touched it once upon a time and felt its gritty surface beneath my fingers. It has a name. Grinding Rock.

I leave the bridge. I walk down the path and stop at the rock. There's a hollow in the stone where Native American women ground their grain. I kneel down and run my hands along the sun-warmed surface. A whisper of memory comes to me on the wind. It carries me back in time. My fingers find shallow scars on the rock. I open my eyes. The scars are barely detectible, yet I know what they are because I put them there. I see a little girl with long chestnut braids, a Band-Aid on her knee, a sunburn on her cheeks. With a dull Boy Scout knife she etches the initials, R. B. I'm that little girl and these should be my initials but they're not. I'm R.D. not R.B.

I reel in the years like the line on a fishing pole. I listen to it sing through time and space. I'm almost back there, balanced on the cusp of memory, when a green truck rattles across the bridge and breaks the spell. Fargo is alone in the car. I have to get back.

As I rise, stiff-kneed from squatting, the silence is upended by blood-curdling shrieks coming from back in the woods. An emergency light pulses in my cop brain and my gun jumps unbidden into my hand. My lost Eden vanishes and I sense danger all around me like I'm being watched from behind the trees.

After a moment of intense confusion I lower my gun. I know that sound. I've heard it before. It's the frenzied squealing of pigs sounding uncannily like humans in distress. Somewhere back in the hollows and groves of Frenchman Wood, pigs are either fighting for dominance at the feeding trough or being slaughtered. Either way, it's an all-out pig panic. I blow out a breath and snap my gun back in the holster.

My heart beating hard in my chest, I trot back to the car, the exhaust from the passing truck still lingering in the air. Fargo is sitting on the back seat with a bewildered look on his face. He wags his tail as I approach. I swing the back door open, wrap my arms around his neck and bury my face in his fluffy brown fur, assuring him—and myself—that everything is okay.

I walk to the driver's side. As I touch the handle I see a bullet hole in the door at chest level. Maybe things aren't so okay after all. It appears to have exited through the open passenger side window. I look around and see no one. It could be a stray bullet from a hunter back in the woods. Then again, it could be a message to limit my explorations to my own backyard.

* * * *

Duane Calhoun was wedged at the center of three boulders forming a half circle. He'd stepped into The Little Papoose to hide along the bank, but had been pulled by the current thirty feet off shore. The force of the water at his back kept him trapped in place, but once the searchers were gone, he'd make every effort to struggle free and try for the bank. At the moment however, he was hopelessly stuck like he had been one way or another his entire life.

Disease had reduced him to skin and bones providing no insulation against the icy rush of water. Going for the river instead of the corn field seemed like a good decision at the time. Just when he felt he couldn't take any more cold, he stopped shivering. How very odd. An unexpected warmth suffused his body, like the false heat you get from certain street drugs.

He might have gotten out of this mess if he hadn't dropped his car keys, if his gun hadn't fallen apart, if that old man hadn't landed a good one to his side. He'd even popped off a shot from Gladys's old Derringer but it went over his head through the open door. If the old geezer had been a better shot he'd be at peace by now.

As the hours ticked away he knew he was dying and Duane started to cry. He wasn't sure why, but when he thought about the early days of his romance with Gladys the tears came. Their romance was good for a while, so very good, but like the song says, it was *much too hot not to cool down*. He'd grown to hate her with a passion equal to the love he'd once held for her, especially after she'd started digging into that old Margie thing. What was he guilty of? What had he done to Gladys that she despised him so? Why did she care if he drank free beer and smoked free cigarettes? She owned a bar for god's sake and sat on a ton of money.

Then, of course, there was the daughter, but he didn't want to think about that. Gladys never knew his secret—or did she? He'd even forgotten the kid's name because it was so different. He hoped she'd forgotten his too. He felt bad about it now, of course. He felt bad about everything—bad about being born—bad about dying.

Tears continued to ran down Duane's face—warm, salty tears falling into the frigid water. He was fading fast, slipping into delirium, his mind rewinding to a night before everything went wrong. He and Gladys lay on a hillside and made love beneath a sky swimming with stars. She called it a Van Gogh sky, like the guy who painted in swirls of silver and blue.

If he did the job right last night, she'd have crossed the Biblical Jordan by now. She'd be waiting for him on the other side and it could be like it was when they first met, love-struck and laughing under a vast ocean of stars. They could start over and do it right this time. It was a comforting thought.

Duane hung on until midnight when he succumbed to hypothermia and cancer and a life poorly lived. The searchers were gone, but Duane no longer had the energy to free himself and struggle to shore. At the last, he died looking up at a sky flaming with stars, reaching out for a hand he only imagined was there.

CHAPTER 13

A VISIT TO THE SHERIFF

Brielle and Charlie headed for town mid-morning. They made one more pass by the Dillon Place and the hardware store before parking in front of the Sheriff's Substation on Main. When they walked in, Undersheriff "Big Mike" Oxenburg waved them to a couple chairs in front of his desk.

"Good morning," he said. "What can I do for you?"

"I'm Brielle Broussard. This is Charlie Chereau. My boyfriend has been missing for two days. His name is Jacob "Coby" Dillon. You may have heard of him. He won the bullriding event at the Abundance Invitational Rodeo."

"I know who he is."

"I need to file a missing person's report."

Mike thought it over a minute.

"That responsibility usually falls to a relative," he said.

"His parents died years ago and his grandmother's memory is failing. Her name is Amity Dillon, out on Dane Road. Now that Coby is unaccounted for there's no one to care for her and she's no longer able to take care of herself."

"I can send a public health nurse out to do an evaluation. Would that make you feel better?

"Yes, thank you."

"I'll get it done today. So, what makes you think your young man is missing? "

"Coby was to start work at the hardware store on Monday, but never showed. No one has seen or heard from him."

"Doesn't he travel with his calf roper friend this time of year?"

"His plan was to quit the rodeo after the Invitational. We had plans to move in with his grandmother on the evening of Rodeo Sunday, but we never connected. If he changed his mind he would have said something to me. I wouldn't feel right if I didn't make an effort to locate him."

Mike looks at Charlie.

"And what's your opinion on all this?"

"Something's wrong. What harm can it do to be on the safe side?"

Big Mike pulled a form from his bottom desk drawer.

"There you go, Miss Broussard. Fill this out and we'll get the ball rolling."

"Thank you."

Brielle began to fill out the form, printing each letter and number neatly, her long dark hair falling on to the paper as she concentrated on each line. She'd barely begun when the front door burst open. Brielle was startled to see Adele and her big brother Archer walk into the station. She pushed her chair back and stood. Charlie rose and stood beside her.

"What are you doing here?" asked Brielle, as Adele approached.

"I might ask you the same."

Big Mike leaned back in his chair and observed the exchange.

"I'm filling out a missing person's report. I haven't seen Coby since the morning of Rodeo Sunday."

"So, your young man stood you up, did he?"

"Put the paper down," said Archer. "Coby's truck is parked outside Bubba's. We'll drive you over."

"That's impossible!" Brielle said.

How did Adele know she was here and that Coby hadn't met her at the bridge?

Brielle looked questioningly at Charlie. He squeezed her hand. He was squarely on her side.

"Come and see for yourself," said Archer. "Don't waste the sheriff's time."

"I'm sorry to have inconvenienced you, Sheriff," said Adele, "but my daughter—well—you know how young girls can be."

Brielle was infuriated by the remark but held her tongue.

With that, Adele grabbed Brielle's arm and ushered her out the door. Charlie and Archer were a step behind them. Charlie touched her shoulder. "I'll call you," he mouthed, under his breath.

Brielle knew that Coby wasn't at Bubba's. Why should Mom or anybody care if she reported him missing?"

Suzette stood on the sidewalk near the Broussard's car as they stepped into the sunlight. Her arms were crossed over her unfettered bosom, her weight slung over one hip. She had a smug *gotcha* look on her face when her eyes met Brielle's. She smiled around the stub of a cigarette.

"Come on, girls. Get in the car," said Adele, throwing the rear car door open for Brielle and Suzette to slide in while she and Archer got in the front seat with her brother behind the wheel.

Brielle stopped abruptly outside the Sheriff's door, then walked purposefully across the sidewalk. She slapped Suzette in the face so hard it could be heard half way down the block. Suzette staggered backward and stumbled off the curb, her cigarette landing in the gutter. She managed to stay on her feet but let out a wounded howl and covered her cheek with her hand.

"That's for being a back-stabbing little tramp," said Brielle. "Find your own way home. I dare you to get in the car with me."

Archer was about to reprimand his sister when he saw the look in her eye and thought better of it.

Charlie climbed in his truck, keyed the engine to life and shifted into gear. As he pulled into the road Suzette ran over and grabbed the passenger side door handle. Charlie leaned across the seat and saw the look of relief on Suzette's face. She turned her head to give Brielle a victorious smirk, but instead of opening the door Charlie punched down the lock and pulled away with a look of satisfaction on his face.

* * * *

Big Mike watched both vehicles leave. That had been quite a display. Something was going on, but he didn't know what. He was about to toss the partially written report, when he changed his mind and dropped it in a drawer. Who knows? She might be back.

He put in a call to Social Services asking if someone would conduct a well-check and health evaluation of Mrs. Dillon. When he finished he put the Out To Lunch sign on the door, climbed in his patrol car and drove across the railroad tracks to Bubba's. He wanted to know who was telling the truth about Coby Dillon.

Mike waded through a sea of motorcycles in the lot out front. By the time he entered the bar the illegal drugs and weapons had been tucked into the nearest hidey-holes. The room smelled of sweat, pot and axel grease. A couple of customers who'd swallowed their joints looked a bit green around the gills. A young blonde woman at the far end of the bar turned her face to the wall.

Mike saw the usual greasy types with beer bellies hanging over their belt buckles, chains around their waists and tattoos around their necks. What he didn't see were pointy boots and cowboy hats. "Relax boys," he said. "All I want is a little information. Any cowboys been in here the last couple days?" he asked.

"Cowboys?" The room filled with laughter. "That bunch of manure fairies?" said the bartender. "We eat them horse jockeys for lunch and spit out the bones."

Everyone in the bar thought that was uproariously funny.

"How about today? Any spurs? Leather chaps?"

"Just like I said. They don't hang here."

It was the truth. This was a biker hangout. Cowboys lived it up at Glad-ys's Bar. The question remained. Why the big lie to keep Brielle Broussard from filing her report?

He walked up to the small blonde facing the wall.

"What's your name, Miss?" She had round finger bruises on her thin arms and a black eye that looked about three days old. She was cute as a kitten under the bruises and looked about twelve years old.

"Mandy Briske," she said, no longer able to pretend he wasn't there.

"Got I.D?"

She produced an I.D. It was real.

"You're twenty-two?" he asked.

"Just like it says."

"You need to come with me."

"Why? I'm legal."

"Because you don't belong here."

Mike turns to Bubba.

"You let this young lady through that door again I'm charging you with assault for all those bruises."

"I didn't do that!"

"I know that, but I'll kick the shit out of you anyway. Got me pal?"

"Loud and clear, Mike."

Back in the parking lot he opened the door and Mandy slid into the passenger seat. Mike got behind the wheel and they bumped back over the railroad tracks toward Main Street.

"Your dad still work at Hillshire Farms?" he asked.

"Yeah. Twenty years now. How did you know?"

"Russ and I went to school together. You wouldn't remember, but I was at your Christening."

"I didn't know that."

They drove for a while in silence. "How about lunch? You could use some meat on your bones."

"Okay."

"Today is brats and sauerkraut day at the Bluebird. Then I'll drive you on home."

"Okay."

"You hang with that crowd and Bubba will be selling those cute little buns of yours to the highest bidder. That what you want?"

"No.You going to tell on me?"

"You going back to Bubba's?"

"No."

"Then I've just developed amnesia."

CHAPTER 14

A HANDFUL OF BONES

A month passed before a fisherman found bones washed up along the shore of The Little Papoose. He didn't think much about it at first. The area was full of predators and any carcass left in the open was bound to be scattered and picked clean in a day or two. Every year, back in the woods during hunting season, he came across bones, many too scattered or crushed to know the animal they'd once belonged to.

Curious, he picked up a bone thicker and longer than the others. Sure looked like it could be a—what's it called?—a femur. He was still mulling the situation over when a skull stared up at him from the shore—the skull of a human animal.

"Holy shit!" He jumped backward three feet.

He left the remains in place and called 911.

Paula arrived in half an hour. She took photos of the bones in situ then brought them back to the lab. She measured the femur to determine the height of the victim and compared the teeth to the x-rays that had been provided by Calhoun's prison dentist. There was a missing lower left molar and a gold cap on an upper right incisor. They were a perfect match to the teeth in the skull.

I drive to the hospital to inform Gladys of the discovery of Calhoun's remains. Her status has been upgraded from critical but stable, to serious. There's every indication that she's going to pull through. The surgeons are having partial success piecing her facial bones back in place, but the presence of a few bone fragments in the frontal cortex cannot be disturbed without endangering her life. The doctors are making slow, measured progress but the risk of infection and stroke are still a concern.

She reads my face the moment I walk in the room.

"They found him," she says, when she sees my expression.

"The bones," I tell her. "Down river."

She shakes her head. "Serves him right for bumping off that Downs girl all those years back."

"There's no one to notify and no one to claim the remains. Paula says he'll be cremated and interred in an unmarked section of the cemetery."

"I don't like that idea," says Gladys, peevishly. "I'll take him."

"What do you mean you'll take him?"

"The remains. I'll claim them."

"Mo-o-m! Are you crazy? You just called him a murderer. He tried to kill you."

"No one's perfect, Robely. Besides, I'm not mad anymore. I should have treated him better than I did all those years ago. I tried marriage four times and blew it every time. I'm just not good at it."

"Yes, but you divorced them—you didn't kill them—that I know of."

Gladys reaches out to me and I take her hand.

"What is it, Mom?"

"I had a dream, Robely, a while back when I was coming out of anesthesia. I saw Duane swimming in an ocean of stars. He held out his hand to me like a swimmer going under for the third time. Isn't that crazy?"

"You're finally rid of him, Mom. Are you sure this is what you want?"

"Yes. And a headstone. Even a dog deserves a little dignity."

If I live to be 100 I'll never figure Gladys out.

"What do you think I should put on the stone?" she asks

I know what I'd put on it, but I keep my opinion to myself.

* * * *

Paula is relieved to put the Calhoun case to bed. She boxed the evidence she'd collected at the bar and tossed it in the morgue incinerator. She'd known Gladys for years as a woman who could walk into a bar full of Cary Grants and walk out with the only Mickey Rourke in the room.

* * * *

A couple weeks after her visit to the Sheriff's Office, Brielle drove Pete's truck to Dane Road one last time. Weeds had taken over the garden, junk mail poking from the mailbox. She walked up the porch steps but there would be no shuffle of slippered feet coming to the door, or a friendly, *Hold your horses*. Brielle went back down the steps with a feeling of emptiness.

As she got into the truck, a man on a tractor came down the road and stopped.

"They took Miss Amity to assisted living in Appleton," he said. "They never could locate her grandson. "Are you a friend of the family?" he asked.

"I used to know her son," she said.

"The Dillons were good neighbors. I miss them."

In the weeks following her visit to the Sheriff's office, Brielle often stood by the bridge looking down at the water or off in the distance. One day in late summer as the leaves were turning, Pete stepped out of the woods and stood beside her. He had a .22 in one hand and held a pair of large grey squirrels by their tails in the other. Their eyes were open and vacant, their silver-grey fur as soft as mink. Father and daughter stood in silence. The breeze ruffling the surface of the water carried a hint of autumn chill.

"You may never find the answer you're looking for, Mon Cher. It blew away on a summer wind."

"I know, Pete."

The sun sank low in the sky and touched the western horizon with a golden fingertip. Pete put an arm around his daughter's shoulders. "My grandfather once said you're not a real person until your heart's been broken at least once."

"You have a funny way of trying to make me feel better."

"Is it working?"

She couldn't help smiling. "Maybe a little."

She loved Adele, but her strongest bond had always been with Pete. He understood her in a deeper way than her mother ever would.

"I know I can't keep coming here, but I can't get past not knowing what happened. I want to let go, but it seems—disloyal."

"You've always been my smartest child," he said. "You'll figure it out in time. For now, why don't you take these squirrels up to Charlie's place? He can dress them out and you two can roast them over the fire pit. It's possible he gets a little lonely up there on the hill."

* * * *

It was late in the season when Frack saw Amity Dillon's obituary in the local paper. He'd met her son Coby and congratulated him on his successful ride the first year he competed in the Invitational. They'd formed a friendship of sorts and he'd been invited to the house a few times when Amity was still well.

It was a drizzly morning. The ladies from Amity's church were in attendance with their husbands, along with a few neighbors and friends he'd never met. Frack scanned the small assembly and wondered why Coby wasn't here.

The casket balanced on ropes over the grave as rain tapped on the canopy above the small gathering. The pastor droned on about ashes and dust. Elderly ladies tossed flowers on the casket.

Standing at the far edge of the gathering was a beautiful girl in a beige rain coat, raindrops glittering in her dark hair, her cheeks wet with tears. He wondered who she was and what her connection was to the Dillon family. As she turned to leave he trotted over and introduced himself.

"I'm Deputy Telusky," he said. "Frank Telusky."

"Brielle Broussard," she replied.

"I don't recall seeing you around town."

"I live with my family in Frenchman Wood."

"A friend of Miss Dillon's?"

"Her son and I were close at one time. I've borrowed my father's truck. I really have to get back."

"Please," he said, "give me a moment. Do you know why Miss Dillon's grandson isn't here?"

Her deep brown eyes searched his face. He could see her hesitation.

"You don't have to be afraid of me, Miss Broussard."

"I haven't seen Coby since the rodeo," she said. "No one has that I know of. We were going to move in together. That's the night he vanished. I knew that something bad had happened but my family doesn't want me getting involved."

"Would you please come to my car so we can get out of the rain? I'd like to hear what you have to say."

* * * *

When Brielle came home from the funeral, Charlie picked her up and they went to Thistle Hill. She'd changed from her black dress into jeans and a soft angora sweater. Her eighteenth birthday had come and gone but it brought little joy.

"So, how did it go?" asked Charlie, as they sat in front of the fireplace. A log collapsed on the grate and sent up a shower of bright sparks.

"They all go pretty much the same," she said. "They dig a hole and put you in it."

He could hear the despondency in her voice.

"Learn anything about Coby?"

"I told my story to a deputy who knew him. He wants to look into his disappearance. Who knows, maybe his crystal ball works better than mine. Everyone at the funeral wondered where he was but nobody knew he was actually missing. Our chance came and went with the missing person's report. If Adele wouldn't let me report him missing, she'd skin me alive if I put up flyers. Archer would only rip them down."

She leaned her head back and looked into the fire.

"Don't let this make you cynical, Brielle. You still have a lifetime of living ahead of you."

She sniffled and brushed away a tear. He sensed more was going on with her than the disappearance of the Dillon boy.

"What? Tell me what's bothering you."

"Charlie, there's something I need to say to you and it doesn't come easy."

"I'm listening. You know you can tell me anything."

"When you married Julie you broke my heart. I want you to know that. I was only twelve, but that's the way I felt. I didn't want anyone to know, especially Julie, especially you. I suppose it shouldn't matter anymore." She smiles sadly. "Pete says you're not a real person unless your heart's been broken at least once. Mine has been broken twice and I'm not even old enough to order a beer. I guess that makes me a real person, but I don't like the way it feels."

"I'm so sorry I hurt you, Brielle."

"Julie seemed to come out of nowhere," she said. "I never saw you two together before you got married. Not once. Not at the family barbecues. Not in church. I was confused. It's like she dropped out of the sky."

"In a sense, she did. Let me tell you what happened. If you don't hear it from me you'll eventually hear it from someone else. Julie was the step-daughter of Pete's older brother Robert. Her mother passed away years ago. Robert lived in Frenchman Wood a while, but there was a disagreement between him and Pete and Robert went back to Canada.

"When Julie developed pancreatic cancer the cutting edge treatment was here at the Mayo Clinic, only a stone's throw across the border in Minnesota, a one day drive from Frenchman Wood. Robert needed my help. I was unmarried, living alone and willing to do what I could. We married so she could have her treatments here without fear of deportation. Unfortunately, her initial diagnosis came too late. The cancer was terminal. The treatments prolonged her life for a while but eventually she lost her battle."

"I'm sorry, Charlie. I'm sorry things ended so badly." She watched the rain fall beyond the window. "I'm usually not like this. I guess it's the funeral—the rain. Sometimes I feel so lost."

Charlie took her by the shoulders and lifted her slowly from the sofa until they were standing only inches apart. He put a finger beneath her chin and raised her face to his. He wiped away a tear.

"I didn't mean to hurt you, Brielle," he said, kissing her gently on the lips. She put her hand on the small of his back and pressed into him. She felt his lips on her throat, the heat of his body through her sweater, his warm breath in her hair. She wanted so desperately to stay, but she knew what would happen between them if she did. And then what? She couldn't survive another disappointment. Ever so slowly she broke the embrace.

"I've got to go," she whispered.

"Please stay."

"I can't. I have to get a few things straight in my mind."

"I'll get my keys."

"No. I want to be by myself just now."

"Brielle—?"

She smiled and touched his cheek. "Good-bye, Charlie." *Charlie my love.*

He watched her walk away until she crossed the bridge in a swirl of rain.

Back at the house she went to her room without a word.

"I wonder what that's all about?" said Adele.

"No you don't," said Pete.

Brielle stood at the window watching the leaves blow past in the wind, still feeling Charlie's warm kiss on her lips. She wondered in that moment if life could be good again or if every day would feel like one more funeral in the rain. To believe—to hope—it was such a dangerous thing.

CHAPTER 15

DEATH ON SUMMER CAMP ROAD

On a day when not much is happening, Frack is assigned traffic duty and I'm off the roster. I'm looking at photos in an old album when I have an idea. I need a key to open a door into my past, into my connection to Frenchman Wood and Grinding Rock. I think I've just found it.

I don't know why it hadn't occurred to me sooner. Maybe it had something to do with the unwelcoming bullet in the car door and the jolting uproar of psychotic pigs.

I pick an old photo from the family album. It's a picture of me, not today, not the grown-up Robely, but the little girl with braids and skinned knees who had once carved initials into a rock.

It's crisp outside with a wind blowing in from the north, the first day I put on my red down jacket and furry boots. Fargo is stretched out across the bedspread. He's snoring contentedly so I let him sleep.

I'm half way to Frenchman Wood when I get a call on my cell from Paula. My first thought is of Gladys. I pull off the road before I answer.

"Paula. Is Gladys okay?"

"She's fine as far as I know, but I have two very sick adult males being treated at General and one deceased seven year old boy I'm looking at as we speak. All are family members, a father, uncle and son. They became sick at a family reunion. I've done the blood work on all three. That makes six confirmed lead poisonings, alcohol related. Four dead in total and two hanging by a thread."

"A seven year old? That's dreadful."

"This time someone is talking. The dead boy's mother. The Lambert family reunion was held at the old campgrounds."

"Paula, I'm on my way to The Wood as we speak. Just tell me what you need."

"Go to the camp at the end of Summer Camp Road. Jolie Lambert, the boy's mother, was unable to locate her father when they left for the hospital. His name is Max Lambert. She thinks he's still up there somewhere."

"I've seen the road. I'm on my way."

"Be careful. I don't know what you might run into up there."

Within half an hour I'm at the bottom of Summer Camp Road. After ten more minutes of steep uphill driving, I arrive at the camp. I get out of the car and walk around. The place has been abandoned for years from the look of it. It's very quiet. There's a cluster of weathered building and platform tents. A rusty fifty gallon barrel is piled high with paper plates, plastic cups and party debris. A stray dog is gnawing on the remains of a roasted pig.

"Max!" I call. "Max Lambert!"

At first I get no response.

I search the buildings and surrounding forest calling his name as I go.

"Over here!" comes a faint reply. I follow the sound and find an elderly man curled on the ground behind a large brick barbecue.

"Where's my family?" he asks.

"Receiving medical care."

"Are they okay?"

"They're in good hands," I tell him. "Mr. Lambert, I'm Deputy Danner. I've been asked to find you and bring you to General. How are you feeling?"

"I have a bad hangover, but I'm not sick like the others. I brought my own bottle and Jolie doesn't drink. The men bought a jar off someone at the bottom of the road. I saw my grandson emptying what little the men left in their glasses but I don't know how much he drank. All three got real sick, real fast. There were others too, but they lit out.

"Can you tell me anything about the person who sold the liquor?"

"Not really. I was already at the camp when word circulated about the French Moonlight. The seller's vehicle couldn't make it up the road so a few of the men walked down."

"Let me help you to the car. I'll put you in the back seat so you can lie down if you want.We're going to the E. R.," I say looping my arm into the crook of his elbow and helping him to his feet.

He asks me several times about the condition of his family. I tell him I don't know, that I was only sent to find him and drive him to the hospital where his daughter is waiting.

* * * *

The next morning I carry out my aborted plan of the previous day.

Paget Corner comes up on my left and I swing into the gravel lot. It's cold and windy. The chairs are no longer on the porch and smoke trickles from a rusted chimney on the roof.

Two elderly men greet me as I walk in.

"You must be the Paget boys," I say.

"Yup! I'm Tom and this young fellow is my brother, Tim."

They both appear to be in their eighties.

"I hear you two were students in this building before they closed the one room schoolhouses."

"That was a long time ago. My dad saw it as the perfect location for a store and he was right."

"You've got a lot of history here. You still sell frog legs?"

"They come in fresh every day,"

"How about three pounds?"

"Coming right up," says Tim, sliding behind the counter.

I pull the photo from my pocket and set it between us.

"Either of you fellows remember this little girl?" I ask.

Tom puts on his bifocals. Tim gets a magnifying glass from under the counter.

"Damned if she don't look familiar. What do you say, Tim?"

They continue to squint at the photo.

"Looks like the little girl used to come in with the Canadian."

Yes!

"Of course, that was a long time ago," says Tom.

"It would have been," I say.

"As I remember, they used to fish the Lost Squaw. She was the cutest little thing. She knew how to put her own worm on the hook. I never saw her after the age of three or so. Not long after that the man stopped coming around."

"Do you recall his name? If he lived in The Wood he'd have come here for his mail."

"It would have been a French name. Most of them are back there. Seems like there's only a few names to go around and they pass 'em back and forth like trading cards, everybody related, however distantly. The same names that were around back then, are still around today."

"Like?—"

"Chevalier. Rochon. Lambert. Help me out Tim."

"Rivette. Petit. L'Beau."

"I'm particularly interested in names starting with B."

"Bonnet. Broussard. Braque."

I scribble everything down in my notebook getting help with the French spellings. I thank them, pay for the frog legs and head for the door.

"What you going to do with all those names, Miss—"

"Robely. Robely Danner. I'm working on family genealogy."

"Well, good luck," says Tom.

"One more thing," I say. "Do you know who owns an old green truck?"

The men, suddenly suspicious, exchange a hesitant glance.

"Lots of folks. I wouldn't know where to start," says Tom. "What brings you out this way, Officer Danner?"

"Looks like I've blown my cover," I say. "Today I'm off the roster, just out for a ride."

"Seen you giving tickets on the highway once," says Tim. "I remember when you made the weekly. You were the first girl sheriff ever hired on. That little girl in the picture sure looks a lot like you."

"Sure does," I say, with a smile. "By the way, you hear anything about bad whiskey coming out of The Wood. Any names come to mind?"

"You trying to get us killed?" says Tom. "Another word and I take those frog legs back," he says, with a chuckle.

"Start with the names you got," says Tim "That's all we got to say on the matter."

I'm almost out the door when he calls me back.

"I just remembered something about the man you fished with. Damned if he didn't have two fingers missing from his left hand."

CHAPTER 16

THE LONG LONESOME TRAIL

Dyce Dean Jackson had come to the end of the rodeo season at a dusty crossroad called Twisted Tree, somewhere in northern New Mexico. The village backed onto a desolate Indian Reservation that was big on sand and low on Indians and didn't rate a fly speck on any road map. It was as good a place as any to rest up before he started back home.

The flat land rolled from horizon to horizon like a dusty carpet lacking the floral design of the vanished summer flowers. It wasn't easy to make a go of it back here. A young Navajo woman sold pottery. An old man charged travelers a dollar to see his two-headed snake. A miner killed rattlesnakes and sold their skins to a company that decorated western hats and belts. Twisted Tree's two day rodeo event brought in a few out-of-towners and Indian's from the Res who hung around a few days, then drifted back among the volcanic chimneys and rocky canyons to tend their goats.

The village had a few commercial establishments. There was Smokey's Western Bar and Grill, the Big Chief Motel, consisting of stucco teepees compliments of the 1950's road trip boom, and the Big Chief Café with a joke-cracking septuagenarian waitress named Darlene.

Dyce had done better this summer than he'd predicted. He'd been out of his league traveling the high end circuits with Coby. He'd made a living at it but he'd never been as good as the young man, even in his own youth.

He was sorry he'd exploded the way he had. Coby didn't deserve it even if he had thrown the first punch. Dyce had made him uncomfortable, invaded his private space, acted like a fool. He'd make it up to him when he got back home, if of course, Coby would talk to him. He thought of writing, but a proper apology could only be given face to face and he never seemed to have a pen and paper at the same time.

Dyce made an effort to keep his drinking in check. He quit the smokes twice and started up again. He coughed more than he used to, but he still looked good on the outside, like a man who could carry a calf through a blizzard or die trying.

Dyce sat in Smokey's at a table for one against the back wall, eyes turned to the falling rain beyond the window. Smokey said it was the first genuine downpour in years. The Indians said it was the Rain Dance that did it. Old folks said it was the Dust Bowl practice of draping dead snakes over barb wire fences.

A petite cotton candy blonde in tight jeans approached Dyce's table. Dyce had removed the second chair so he could drink in solitude, but the friendly ladies of Twisted Tree were undeterred.

Here it comes, he thought, finishing off his sixth beer of the night.

"I know you!" bubbled the blonde. "You used to be the Marlboro Man, right?" He didn't bother arguing the point. There had actually been several men who had assumed the role but most of them had died of COPD, compliments of the product that made them famous back in the day. When asked politely he signed his name to the cover of her Western Horseman magazine. She'd never know the difference and neither would anybody else.

"I could pull up another chair," she said, "if you feel like a little conversation."

"I wish I could Miss, but I gotta go tend my horse. It was a pleasure meeting you however." He got up and gave Smokey a ten as he passed the bar. "See the lady gets a couple drinks," he said.

"Sure 'nuff, Dyce. I'm still holding a hundred bucks for the first lady gets you in the sack."

"Tell 'em I'm not worth the effort. I left my Viagra back in Nueva Laredo."

Smokey's laughter followed Dyce through the back door.

"What's his story?" said the blonde picking up her first complimentary drink. "I must be losing my touch."

"Looks to me like a man who's nursing a broken heart," said Smokey. "If *you* can't get it done, no one can."

Smokey was almost right—but not quite.

It was near midnight when Dyce approached the stable where Gunpowder was bedded down. A young man stood beneath a blue light that dropped on a cord from the overhang above the boardwalk. Cold blue rain spiraled in the wind and lightning branched along the far horizon.

With twenty feet between them, and half a tank of beer on board, the kid looked so much like Coby that an arrow of pain shot across Dyce's chest.

As Dyce moved closer, the young fellow took on a bit more age. He looked somewhere in his late 20's or early 30's. It was his slight frame and poor-boy persona that made him seem younger at first glance. He had a cocky James Dean slouch and flipped a rope into a knot in mid-air like Dean did in the movie *Giant*. Dyce had known a handful of guys who'd replicated that trick—not an easy one to master—but none who'd done it with the seamless nonchalance of the blonde-haired kid in front of him. He wore a tattered cowboy hat and badly scuffed boots like he'd fought his whole life to keep his belly full and his dignity intact.

Curiosity—or was it something else?—drew Dyce closer.

He watched as the kid hung the rope on a nail and tapped out a cigarette. He scraped a match but it was too damp to spark.

Dyce moved in and lighted the cigarette. The flame from his Zippo reflected off a pair of drop-dead blue eyes. There were delicate crow's feet at the corners, like the kid spent his life searching the horizon for something that never materialized. Thunder rumbled across the sky and rain drummed on the metal roof of the stable.

"Waiting for someone?"

"Nope," said Dyce. "Just come to check on my horse."

"I'm Kai Furlong. It's a surfer name, but I've never seen the ocean."

"Then you're safe from sharks. I'm Dyce Jackson."

"I know. The calf roper. I know the name of every person for fifty square miles."

Dyce smiled. "Really? All thirty of them?"

Kai smiled back. "I know their secrets too, even the one's they keep from themselves."

"That's quite a talent."

"I was born on the seventh day of the seventh month. A fortune teller called it an auspicious juxtaposition of numbers. My gift is knowing what people think before they think it."

"In that case, you'd know what I'm thinking?"

"That's easy. You're thinking I know something you don't want other people to know."

Kai took a long drag from his cigarette and blew a smoke ring that dissolved in the wind.

"That applies to everyone on earth if you dig deep enough," said Dyce. "Everyone has something they don't want other people to know." He took a cigarette from his pack, but when he reached for his lighter Kai stopped his hand with a firm grip that sent a ripple of electricity up his arm.

"No sense wasting fire," said Kai, riveting Dyce with those fire-blue eyes. Kai guided Dyce's cigarette to his own. Two cinders glowed red in the wet blue night. Dyce took a deep drag to keep it lit and reclaimed his hand.

"You smoke Gold Coast?" said Dyce, referring to the cheapest smokes on the market. "You might as well smoke candy wrappers for all the charge you get out of them."

"What do you mean? Two Golds, back to back, are as good as one Camel Straight."

"Then they're not cheap anymore."

"Don't go getting technical on me? It makes my head hurt." An ash blew from Kai's cigarette. "Smokey thought you'd leave the bar with Barbie Fuller tonight. She's a pretty hot number in these parts, the only girl in Twisted Tree without a drop of Indian blood."

"She's a winner all right, but she's not my type."

"Neither were the others. I knew that before they slipped their Day After pills into their purses."

"Aren't you the know-it-all?" The kid was either psychic or a carnival trickster in a cowboy get-up.

"Don't look so edgy," said Kai, laughing out loud. "It's not like I'm going to run home and tell your mother."

Before he knew what was happening, Kai had stuck his toe in a door that Dyce hadn't intended to open, psychologically speaking that is.

"You live around here?" asked Dyce, changing the trajectory of the conversation.

"Sort of," said Kai. "We got 40 acres two miles west, but the bank wants it back. We prayed for rain but it came too late. First the farm died. Then Mom passed and Dad cut out. There's just me and Aunt Nel, but the doc says she won't see spring."

"That's a damn sad story, kid." Dyce took a drag on his cigarette, studied the kid's face. "Is it true?"

"Wish it wasn't."

"Then what?"

"By the time it's over, I'll have figured something out. I always do."

"Maybe your dad will ante in again."

Kai kicked up a divot of dirt with the raggedy toe of his boot. "Let me tell you about my old man." He stared at his boots for a few seconds, then looked up. "He heard rumors about me when I was fifteen. He almost beat me to death with the buckle end of his belt for the embarrassment I caused him, him being this macho bad-ass cowboy and all." In that brief moment his eyes seemed wet and softly gray, windows opening onto the rain. "The only thing he ever memorized from the Scriptures was about sparing the rod and he made good use of it."

He huffed a laugh. "A dangerous lot them Bible thumpers. Turned me away from the church for good."

Dyce flicked away the stub of his cigarette. "You standing out here for any particular reason?" he asked.

"I'm waiting for my engine to cool down. It's the truck behind Smokey's with the crooked tail pipe. It gets hot after about fifteen minutes on the road. When I'm driving I expect the head to blow any second." There was a slight waiver in his laugh, a note of melancholy slipping through the bravado. "Where you going to spend the night?"

"Like there's a choice?" said Dyce, popping a laugh. "Teepee Seven.

You're lucky number, kid. Tomorrow I head back home."

"Where's that?"

"Abundance, Wisconsin. I know the name of every milk cow for ten square miles."

Kai laughed. "You got a place of your own?"

"Fifty acres. The land is good but the house needs a lot of fixing. When the weather's good I'm on the road. When winter comes it's too late to worry about it."

"My dad always said I was good with a hammer. It's about the only nice thing he ever said to me. You like it there?"

"Wisconsin? It's okay if you can take the winters. There's good hunting and fishing, a lot of lakes and trees."

"It's nice having someone to talk to. There aren't a lot of people out my way. Why don't you load up your horse and spend the night at my place unless you got a special thing for stucco teepees. It'll save you sixty bucks and you can take off for home in the morning. I'll put your horse up in the barn."

"I don't feel right imposing on your aunt and all."

"Listen Dyce, you've got the high desert lonesomes same as me or we wouldn't be standing here in the midnight rain like two wet puppies. My aunt has the main house. My bunkhouse is out back. I'll make us a fire and we can dry our clothes."

Dyce considers his options.

"Okay. How about I follow you out? If your engine explodes on the way we'll have a second set of wheels."

Within the hour, Dyce and Kai were settled in, their clothes drying on a line below the ceiling. Except for the rain on the roof and the crackling pine logs in the stove it was very quiet.

Kai took a couple glasses from a shelf and poured them each three fingers of dark magic from a bottle.

"It's called Mudslide," he said, "in honor of the storm that introduced us."

They clicked glasses and lay back on couch pillows they'd tossed on the floor in front of the stove. They drank slowly and Dyce felt the ropes of muscle relax in his neck and shoulders. How long since he'd really relaxed? He can't remember back that far.

It was Kai who broke the silence. He spoke quietly, flames wavering in his blue eyes.

"What was his name?"

Dyce hesitated, but only for a beat.

"Coby."

"And things went sideways?"

"Things never went anywhere at all."

CHAPTER 17

FROM TREASURE TO TROUBLE

Now that school was back in session, Anton and Henri lived for the last golden weekends of autumn. On a mellow Saturday morning they raced through the woods toward the bridge, their colorful bobbers dancing on the tips of their fishing poles.

They were tired of being frightened by the infamous legends of the Rivettes, most of which went back to the old days of their great-granddad. They hadn't seen old Devil Rivette since he took sick and Sabine was so ornery she scared people off.

Even though most of Charlie's property was on the far side of the creek, an acre this side of the dog fence was an extension of his land and Anton and Henri had every right to play here.

By noon they had five fat trout between them, enough for an evening fish fry if nobody got too greedy. They climbed up the bank and ate their lunch beneath an oak tree on the safe side of the dog fence. Today the dogs must have been up at the house because there was none of the ritual growling and fence-lunging. The boys laid back and gazed into the treetops. When the wind whipped up a thousand leaves spiraled downward in a shower of gold.

"I love the woods," said Anton. "I'm never moving away."

"No place else would have us," said Henri, and they both giggled.

"Maybe in a few years Pete and Charlie will bring us into the family business."

"We're not supposed to know about the family business."

"It's not like it's a secret."

When the wind calmed, things grew quiet except for the birds and the murmur of water. Anton sat up.

"Do you hear that?"

"What? said Henri.

"Listen." Both boys got to their feet.

"I hear it," said Henri. "A buzzing."

"More like a humming," corrected Anton. "It's coming from the shed beside the Rivette's water pump."

They moved closer to the fence but there wasn't much to see.

"Look there," said Anton.

"What?"

"There's an orange electrical cord running from the house to the shed."

"So what?"

"That's where they keep the old farm machinery and non op cars. I snuck in there a long time ago. There was no need for electricity. You know how tight the Old Devil is with his money."

"Could be a hundred reasons." said Henri. "Maybe they have a still."

"A still doesn't need electricity. They have three back in the ravine. I found them months ago. I thought of busting them up for the fun of it, but they'd think Pete did it, so I let them be."

"You sure seem to be well-informed," said Henri.

"I like to explore after everyone's asleep."

"On the Rivette's property?"

"Sometimes, but not too close to the house because of the dogs."

"Pete would nail your hide to the barn door."

"I'm not going to get caught."

"Neither was John Dillinger."

"He didn't get caught. He got shot."

"I don't see that as a big win."

"I wanna get into that shed."

"It's too risky," said Henri.

"We need to come at night."

"You're forgetting about the dogs?"

"I'll think of something."

"Come on, let's get out of here."

As they stepped back from the fence Henri's toe kicked something out from under the leaves. He knelt down and picked up what looked like a moldy piece of leather. He was about to throw it into the creek when he realized what he had. He examined the item more carefully and couldn't believe their luck. They picked up their gear and ran for home.

* * * *

Dyce woke and dressed quietly as Kai slept. He resisted the urge to smooth the lock of blonde hair out of the boy's eyes for fear of waking him. Good-byes were awkward. Best to just go.

He stopped this side of the door. He could see the once-upon-a-time child in Kai as he slept, the worked-out, done-in farm kid who was losing both his farm and his family. Looking down at Kai's battered boots put a lump in his throat.

He drove north under a polished blue sky. The next day he stopped at a small town and filled up on gas, pancakes and coffee. He left a tip and walked down the sidewalk to Billy's Western Store.

"I'd like a pair of boots for a friend of mine," he said.

"Work boots or parade boots?" asked the proprietor.

"Work."

"Tony Lamas been around since 1911. It's what my granddaddy always swore by."

"Sounds good to me."

Dyce decided on a beautifully stitched black and turquoise boot that had the wonderful smell of fine leather. He could see Kai now, strutting around, flipping his rope, looking very James Dean cool.

"How about a hat to go with it?" said Billy.

"Whatcha got?"

"On the high end we got a Stetson Yukon for two hundred and ninety-eight dollars."

"Holy shit! That's what I paid for my horse trailer."

Billy laughed. "We also have an excellent Cavendar Ranch Straw with a Cattleman's Crown for eighteen dollars and seventy four cents."

"I'll take it. Here's my friend's name and P.O. Box. You mind mailing it for me?"

"No problem. What size on the boots?" asked Billy.

"Can I use your phone?"

"Sure. I have free long distance as long as it's in the lower forty-eight."

Dyce dialed the Big Chief Cafe and Darlene picked up.

"Hey darling, it's Dyce. Sorry I didn't have a chance to say good-bye. I'm in a shop in a town called—"

"Friendly, Scorpion, Nebraska," said Billy.

"Scorpion, Nebraska, and I need some information."

"Hell baby, there goes my hundred dollars. I was next in line after Barbie Fuller."

"I'm sorry to be such a major disappointment to you ladies."

"What do you need, honey?"

"You know Kai Furlong, right?"

"The kid who knows everybody's name within 50 square miles?"

He could almost see her rolling her eyes.

"Yes that one. I need his boot size."

"He ain't got nothin' on me, mister. Did I mention I know everyone's boot size in the state. Size 10. I like that boy. He deserves better than what he got."

"Now he gets a pair of boots."

"You're a stand-up guy, Dyce. Will I see you next year?"

"I might come by for a visit but I'm through competing."

"Can I ask you a question?" she said.

"Shoot."

"Does he get the one hundred dollars? It ain't no secret about Kai you know."

Dyce pauses, but he's not backing away this time, not like he has his whole life.

"Tell Smokey to give him the money."

"That's my man, Dyce. Have a safe journey home."

* * * *

Ten miles outside of Abundance, Dyce slowed to a crawl when he saw a teenage girl with long blonde braids on a beautiful blood bay mare. Her horse looked a lot like Coby's horse Chili. He pulled ahead of her and waited on the shoulder until the girl caught up.

"You having engine trouble, mister?" she asked, reining to a stop.

"No, Miss, just taking a breather. That's a beautiful horse you're riding."

"Thank you."

"What's her name?"

"Wild Flower. She didn't have a name when Daddy bought her."

"Recently?"

"Early summer. She's not for sale if that's what you're thinking."

"One horse is enough for me," he said, gesturing toward the horse trailer. He get her at auction?"

She nodded.

"Midland?"

"Prairie Dells. Why?"

"No special reason."

She was becoming wary but he pressed on.

"Must have cost a pretty penny, a fine horse like that."

"Must have. I got her for my 16th birthday."

"You're a lucky girl. I'm Dyce Jackson. I live in Abundance.

"Why are you asking so many questions?"

"She looks like a horse that belonged to a friend."

"She's mine now."

A whinny and an excited clatter of hooves came from the back of Dyce's horse trailer. Wild Flower pricked up her ears and wouldn't stop snorting and tossing her head. It was apparent that the horses knew one another. This was Coby's mare.

"I have to go," said the girl.

"Ever have her scanned for a chip?"

"If I'm late I'll get in trouble." She turned and galloped away. A quarter mile up the road she trotted up a long driveway that led to a big white house. The name on the mailbox read G. Magneson.

* * * *

Anton and Henri dumped their fishing gear in the corner of the porch and raced into the kitchen, breathless with excitement. Henri was so pumped up he didn't notice the burrs tangled in his hair. Adele turned from warming a pot of stew on the wood stove.

"What in the world has gotten into you two?" she said. "You look like you're being chased by the *loup garou*."

"You'll never guess what we found by the creek," said Henri, handing Adele his treasured find. She took it from his hand very gingerly. It was a crusty piece of leather covered with a thin patina of mold.

"It doesn't look like much," she said, a bit of mold rubbing off on her fingers. She wet a paper towel and rubbed at the surface. The small rectangular piece of leather had a hand-tooled border. She turned it over and rubbed the other side until, little by little, the barely discernable image of a bucking bull appeared.

Adele saw the fine line where two crusty edges of leather came together and carefully separated them to reveal what the boys had already discovered. They couldn't wait to see the look of excitement on their mom's face. Without fully removing the contents, she counted eight one hundred dollar bills.

"Now we have our pony money!" squealed the twins jumping up and down.

Adele opened the wallet wider and saw a laminated driver's license, dirty but unaffected by the elements. It's the first time she'd seen Coby Dillon's handsome, young face or known his full name was Jacob Lee Dillon. The color drained from her face. The twins were puzzled by her expression.

"What is it Mom? What's wrong?"

"Have you boys looked inside?" she asked.

"Yes, we counted the money."

"Did you see anything else?"

"No. We don't care about anything else."

She flung the stove door wide and tossed the wallet into the flames. The twins began to wail. Anton tried to snatch it from the fire but the wallet had already shriveled to half its size. He pulled back his hand with a yelp and Adele slammed the door with a metallic clang.

"Mom!" they screamed. "Mom, what are you doing?"

"Where did you find this?"

"Near the fishing hole behind the dog fence."

"On Charlie's property?"

"Yes."

"You're not to speak of this to anyone."

"That was our pony money," wailed Anton.

She grabbed each boy by an arm and shook them severely until their heads bobbled back and forth on their skinny little necks.

"There was never a wallet. There was never money. You are never to breathe a word of this—ever! Promise me." The boys were wide-eyed with fear. "Promise!" she snapped.

"I promise," said Anton, scared at the look in his mother's eyes.

"And you?" she said, focusing on Henri.

"I promise too," he said, tears running down his cheeks.

"Enough sniveling, Henri. Fetch me the can of lard and I'll get those burrs out of your hair."

That night in their beds, Anton turned to Henri.

"After things settle down I'm going back," he whispered.

"You mean to the dog fence?"

"Mom said we couldn't talk about it. She never said we couldn't go back."

"I'm coming too," said Henri.

On the other side of the wall Pete and Adele talked in hushed voices.

"Tell me you had nothing to do with that boy's disappearance," said Adele, still shaken by what the boys had found.

"You know better than to ask me that."

"How about Charlie? How did he know Brielle was stranded in the woods when she was supposed to have left with the boy hours before? After all, the wallet was found on his property."

"For god sake Adele! He was hunting with the rest of us that evening."

"Yes, but you don't know what he did after the hunting party broke up. You know how Charlie feels about Brielle. God only knows what a man would do to get the woman he wants."

"Charlie has never been a hot-head. He may be the only sane man in the family."

"I think that young cowboy made it to the bridge, but I don't think he got out of the woods alive."

"Adele, your imagination is running away with you. If that's true he couldn't have driven away in his truck. Ever think of that?"

"I can't explain it, but one thing is certain. This was no robbery or there wouldn't be eight hundred dollars in the wallet. There are only so many motives for murder and jealousy is high on my list."

"For heaven's sake, woman! We don't know that there *was* a murder. Where's the body? Where's the evidence? Maybe he simply lost his wallet."

"That would still put Coby at the bridge and Charlie in the woods. What are we going to tell Brielle?"

"Nothing! We keep our mouths shut—for now," said Pete, "I need time to think this through."

CHAPTER 18

WHERE IS COBY DILLON?

I drive home from the library and cover the dining room table with photo-copied plat maps.

Frack walks behind my chair and looks over my shoulder.

"What are you up to?" he asks. "That looks like the plat of Frenchman Wood."

"It's a portion of it. I want to know who owns the properties nearest the bridge over the Lost Squaw."

"Does this have to do with the moonshiners Paula was talking about?"

"It's about the stills, but it's also about me." I'm looking for surnames that start with B."

"I'm a little lost here. How is this about you?"

"When I was walking near the bridge someone put a bullet in my driver's side door. I was nowhere near the car so I decided not to make a federal case of it."

"I didn't see a bullet hole," said Frack. "You're sure you're not making this up to get attention? Have I been neglecting you lately?"

"Not lately and not ever. I stuck a piece of gum in the hole and painted it over. I didn't want you to worry. If someone wanted me dead, I'd already be dead"

Frack kissed me on the back of the neck and pulled a chair next to mine.

"That was pretty sneaky. I thought we were supposed to tell each other everything."

"You're right. I'm sorry."

"Did you retrieve the bullet?"

"It wasn't possible. It exited through the open passenger side window. I'd have to have gone through an acre of poison ivy with a dental pick."

"Any idea who did it?"

"The only vehicle that passed was a green truck but I never saw the driver. It could have been a stray shot from back in the woods or a suggestion that I limit my snooping to my own backyard. It's impossible to know."

"When did this happen?"

"The day I picked Fargo up from the vet. I was curious. If I was going to look for evidence of stills I wanted to get a feel for what it was like back in The Wood."

"What does this have to do with names that start with B?"

"This is where things get a little odd. The deeper I got in the woods, the more I felt that I'd been there before. I walked straight to a large boulder on the far side of the creek, the hollowed out kind the Indian women used for grinding grain. I knew what I'd find before I got there. Scraped into the rock were the initials RB. I remember putting them there when I was very small—a long time ago—almost beyond memory. I'm R.B. or I was at one time. I'm certain of it. The elderly gentlemen at Paget Corner said I used to come in the store with a man who had two fingers missing. That had to be my father. I have to start somewhere so I'm starting with B. You have a better suggestion?"

"I'd suggest you to stop poking around before something bad happens. You think it's worth taking a bullet to find a guy who might not want to be found?"

I kiss him on the cheek.

"I'll let you know. Besides, the shot wasn't about the B."

Frack shook his head.

"I noticed Wheezy left you a message on the machine," says Frack. "How's he doing?"

"He's healing, but it's not going to happen overnight. When the bar re-opens he'll need a second bartender to back him up. I don't know if Gladys will be able to run it again, and if she does, I don't know when that will be. She might decide to sell."

"I guess we'll have to wait and see. Can I change the subject for a minute?"

"Please do."

"Ever hear the name Coby Dillon?"

"Sure. The bullrider. I saw him in action when I ran security for the rodeo. Why?"

"Nobody seems to know where he is."

I push the maps aside and give him my full attention.

"What do you mean? Wouldn't he be on the circuit?"

"Even if he was he'd be back by now. His girlfriend said they were going to settle down together, that he was starting a new job at the hardware store the day after Rodeo Sunday. They planned to move in with his grandmother but he never showed. The girlfriend's name is Brielle Broussard. I met her at Amity Dillon's gravesite."

"Broussard. That was among the names the Paget brothers gave me as being a long- established family in Frenchman Wood. It also starts with a

B."

"That and a dozen others. Don't start getting carried away. Anyway, Miss Broussard said she started filling out a missing person's report but her family didn't want her getting involved. She won't let it go until she knows what's happened to him."

"I don't blame her. What if he wasn't ready to settle down? It wouldn't be the first time a guy got cold feet."

"They were moving in together the evening he vanished. I didn't know him well, but he seemed a steady type."

"You've certainly heard about women being left at the altar. It's not exactly a new way of breaking up, although now I hear they do it by text message. Tell me about Miss Broussard. What is she like?"

"She strikes me as having both feet on the ground. She's on the quiet side. About 16 or 17. She's smart. She jumped a grade and graduated high school early."

"She's very young to be settling down."

"That's true, but she seemed more grown-up than most girls her age. She attended the funeral to show her respects to Coby's grandmother. She scanned the crowd hoping to see Coby. Of course, he wasn't there. No one's seen him since June."

"June!" I say, pushing the maps aside. "Let's go see what Mike remembers."

* * * *

When we enter the station Mike is rubbing the stains out of the coffee pot and setting up the machine for the next day."

"Hey, Mike. Gotta minute?" says Frack.

"Something going on?" he asks.

"You remember a girl came into the station a while back. She wanted to file a missing person's report."

"Sure. Brielle Broussard. She was with a somewhat older fellow I took for a cousin, maybe an uncle—who knows with those people? It was about her missing boyfriend, but her family dragged her away before she could finish filling out the form. They told her Coby was drinking at Bubba's. Out of curiosity I drove over after they left, but he wasn't there, just the usual biker crowd."

"What do you make of it?" I ask.

"Other than the fact her family lied to her, your guess is as good as mine." Mike opened a drawer and pulled out the unfinished report. Frack and I went over it together, not that there was much to see. *Jacob Lee Dillon. DOB.4-10-96 Height: 5' 10" Weight 155. Place of Residence. 17034 Dane Road. Last known sighting. Rodeo Sunday in the company of—"*

"Oh, that's great!" said Frack. "It would sure be nice to have that name."

"When Coby left the fairgrounds he was being tailed by a man in a red truck pulling a horse trailer," I said. "I remember because he nearly hit me in the head with his side mirror. That doesn't mean that he caught up with him or that he was the last person to see him, but he pissed me off so I wrote down his license plate number. His name is Dyce Dean Jackson, calf roper."

I take out my notebook, rip out the page with the license number and hand it to Mike.

"Wanna run it?"

"Do I ever." Mike opens his computer and logs on. He begins tapping away.

"So finish your story, Mike. What happened when her family arrived?"

"They escorted her out. I watched through the window. A girl named Suzette Rochon was standing at the curb. She's one resident of The Wood whose acquaintance I've made on more than one occasion. I've picked her up twice for solicitation and three times on a drunk and disorderly. She gave Miss Broussard a snotty look and Miss Broussard walked over and slapped the cigarette out of her mouth. It was a lovely sight to behold. When they drove away Miss Rochon was standing in the street having a hissy fit."

"That's interesting," says Frack.

The phone rings. Within seconds all five buttons light up.

"Oh, now what!" grumbles Mike. "Can't a guy get any peace around here?"

I laugh out loud. "If you wanted peace you should have been a mailman."

Mike grabs a line and puts it on speaker. The Bubba crowd is going at it with baseball bats. All three of us fly out the door.

* * * *

Dyce's back was in knots by the time he pulled in front of his spread on Meadow Road. His neck was stiff and his bad leg ached from hours behind the wheel. He drove through the main gate and parked in front of the barn as the shadows lengthened and the orange ball of sun sank below the pine trees.

He opened the tailgate and backed Gunpowder slowly down the ramp, then walked him in wide slow circles to work out the stiffness from the long hours in the trailer.

After fifteen minutes Gunpowder tossed his head and broke into a graceful trot. Dyce opened the gate to the two acre pasture and unfastened the halter. Gunpowder ran the perimeter of the fence line, his silver mane and tail rippling in the wind. He'd been gelded later than most horses and you could still see the stallion thundering through his blood.

Dyce filled the trough with fresh water and the manger with hay. The first evening star hung above the horizon and an owl hooted from a nearby tree. Gunpowder galloped to the top of a knoll He tossed his mane and trumpeted his freedom to the sky.

Dyce entered the house through the back door. It had the closed up smell of dead air, dust and mice. He snapped on a table lamp, lit the thermostat on both the wall heater and the water heater and opened the windows until the dust burned off the elements. When the air smelled fresh he settled in his recliner and finished off a six pack of beer. He fell asleep wearing one boot, his cigarette dying between his fingers.

CHAPTER 19

DIGGING FOR TROUBLE

Adele lay in bed with her long hair fanned out across the pillow. In the glow of the night light she looked softer and younger than her years. Pete spoke to his wife in French, as the wind whooshed around the corners of the house, muffling any words that might be detected by little ears pressed to the other side of the bedroom wall.

"Charlie and I dismantled the still this afternoon," he said.

"What? I never thought I'd hear those words coming from you."

"We've opted out of the booze business. We smashed up what we could and buried the pieces at various sites on the properties. It's time to quit while we're ahead."

"You mean before you're caught."

"You could put it that way. We'll make it on the livestock and the garden. I think I'll start making cradles and lawn furniture again. They always sold well."

"I like that idea," she said. "Brielle can't sleep until you and Charlie are home safely from your runs. She'd never interfere, but it's hard on her. Is Charlie okay with your decision?"

"It was actually his idea. He makes good money with his sawmill. I think the days of French Moonlight are coming to an end anyway. We're not the only ones phasing out. I feel trouble brewing and I don't want to be caught up in it. Someone in The Wood is using lead-contaminated fittings on their still. There have been fatalities, how many I can't say. I'd like to blame it on Devil Rivette, except his French Moonlight has always been as pure as ours—pure as spring water."

Adele laughs. "Except spring water doesn't kick you in the head like a wall-eyed mule."

"That's its job, woman. A man needs a kick in the head every now and then. Anyway, Devil might try to shoot us on a midnight run, but he'd never sell bad whiskey. It's his religion and he lives by its commandments."

"That's quite a character reference," said Adele, unable to keep a straight face.

Pete couldn't help laughing along with her.

"Another reason I'm quitting the game is our boys. I don't want them following in my footsteps. There's a bigger world out there and I want them to be a part of it. I hate to admit it, but I think we were wrong making Brielle's young man unwelcome. If we'd been more cordial, asked him up to the house that night, he might not be—unaccounted for."

Adele squeezed her husband's hand.

"Speaking of cordiality, Charlie got a letter from Robert. Before the snow flies he's coming down to visit Julie's grave. He's had more than his share of disappointments, his wife dying those many years ago and now his stepdaughter. Some people have more than their share of sorrow."

"Oh, come on! It's not that bad. He owns a successful lumber supply in British Colombia," said Pete. "Makes money hand over fist from what I hear."

"Don't be so dense! I'm talking about personal things. I hope you can make peace with your brother after all these years."

"I doubt it. He did a lot of stupid things when he was here last—that unsuitable woman for one."

"You're impossible, Pete! That was almost 30 years ago," she said, giving him an elbow jab. "Don't bother kissing me good-night if that's the way you're going to be."

"I had a lot more than a kiss in mind, Mon Cheri."

* * * *

The night was unseasonably warm, the last gasp of heat before the cold settled in for good. Brielle opened her bedroom window and leaned on the sill letting the night air stream through her hair and flutter the hem of her long white nightgown.

Coby was gone and never coming back. It was the secret her parents were trying so hard to keep from her. She didn't know what they knew or how they knew it, but they avoided meeting her eyes and quietly left the room when she entered, lending the house the flower-scented hush of a funeral home.

If Coby were to suddenly appear it would be too late to recapture the brief magic they'd shared before the great mystery of his disappearance. That didn't mean that she would stop trying to find out what happened to him on that stormy summer night that now seemed so long ago.

She closed her eyes and imagined Coby as a young eagle who'd landed on her hand. She drew a breath and gently blew his winged spirit to a peaceful place beyond the clouds.

When she opened her eyes she found she was breathing more easily. Her heart was more content. She glanced at the distant house on Thistle Hill where a porch light burned into the night. The light flickered off and back on as if Charlie knew she was watching from her window.

Brielle flicked the wall switch and returned his greeting.

"Goodnight, Charlie," she whispered.

* * * *

While Henri waited at the edge of the woods, Anton went around the corner of the barn into the smokehouse. He returned with a big chunk of pork shoulder and hid it in his empty creel. It was a mellow afternoon and the twins decided it was safe to return to the Lost Squaw for another look around.

"Mom's going to kill us if she finds out," said Henri. "That meat is enough for Sunday dinner, even if Charlie comes."

"It's for the Rivette's dogs, dummy. It will shut them up while we search for more money."

"If there was more money it would have been in the wallet, stupid."

"We won't know that until we've gone over the ground inch by inch. Anything you'd rather be doing right now, go do it."

Of course, Henri followed his brother to the field above the Lost Squaw

They put their fishing gear beneath the shade tree and it wasn't but a minute before the three skinny hounds came barking and lunging at the wire fence. The moment they hit the wires they were knocked backward by their shock collars. Anton cut off a satisfying amount of meat for each dog. He tossed the chunks over the fence and watched the pork disappear in a gulp or two.

The dogs could still smell the smoked pork in the creel, but this time they lay down beside the fence, whining and begging more politely. Every time they became restless the boys gave them smaller tidbits until they were eating out of their hands, ears forward, tails wagging. When the meat was gone and they'd had their fill the dogs curled up and went to sleep.

Now the twins could search without the annoyance of the dogs. Although Devil stayed mostly indoors with his ailment, the boys were on alert. They didn't want to tangle with Sabine. She was unpredictable and some people in The Wood said she had a screw loose.

The boys searched through the leaves, sifted the dirt around the trees, even dug around in the sand along the bank of the bayou. They picked up every item that caught their interest as if they were seasoned anthropologists. Henri found several beautiful stones for show and tell. He took pride in knowing the difference between igneous, metamorphic and sedimentary rock.

Into their creel went a narrow and knuckley chicken bone, the heel of a boot, some small metal buttons and square nails caked with rust. Henri found a human tooth in the reeds beside the bayou and tossed that in too. Maybe they could use it to trick the tooth fairy into leaving money under their pillows. Sadly, they found no treasure in the form of cash.

It was Anton who noticed a glint of metal in the leaves just this side of the fence. As he got closer the hum coming from the shed grew loader, the orange cord still plugged in at the back of the house. He was only feet from the dogs but they were fast asleep like fat men after a feast.

Anton bent over and brushed away the leaves. The ground around his feet was peppered with buckshot. Within seconds Anton stood up, waving a dirt-caked piece of oval metal, heavy and bigger than the palm of his hand. He and Henri raced to the creek and washed their newly unearthed treasure. It was a fancy belt buckle. At center was the raised image of a rider on a bucking bull.

"Wow! This has got to be worth big bucks," said Anton.

Henri agreed that it was truly magnificent.

"I'll tell you one thing," said Anton. "It's not going into the wood stove. I know exactly how to turn this baby into cash."

"A bull on the wallet?" said Henri, thoughtfully. "A bull on the buckle? Sounds to me like—"

"Just shut up, Henri. Don't go complicating things. There's an old French law that says *finders keepers.*"

"Are you sure?"

"Would I say it if it wasn't true?"

The Rivette's screen door banged against the back of the house and Sabine Rivette with shotgun in hand came out back in her floppy hat and shapeless work boots, the long leather laces dragging in the dust.

The boys hid in a blackberry thicket behind the trees.

"Snockered again," whispered Henri, suppressing a giggle.

Sabine looked around. She had the instincts of a predator but her eyesight was poor. Some people said it didn't matter because she had eyes in the back of her head.

It angered Sabine that her hounds were sleeping on the job. Her leg shot out to kick the biggest dog awake but she lost her balance along with one of her boots. She went down hard on her butt, the shotgun discharging like a bomb. The dogs jumped to their feet, yelping and whimpering, their ears ringing painfully.

When Anton and Henri realized that no living creature had been blown to bits, they rolled on the ground in silent laughter until their sides ached. After the old witch struggled to her feet and returned to the house, the boys gathered their treasures and ran laughing all the way home.

CHAPTER 20

LOOKING FOR ANSWERS

The morning after the biker brawl, Frack and I wake with multiple abrasions and contusions. Frack has a lovely black eye. I have a bump on my head and a sprained left index finger. We bonded over our wounds and made love like two porcupines—very carefully.

Mike, despite that extra 30 pounds, turned out to be a natural born scrapper. Like a rotund Bruce Lee, he laid out five of the more aggressive chain-swinging, knife-wielding combatants without suffering a single serious wound. Two of the more seriously injured bikers were cuffed and taken to the hospital after the ruckus. Another three were thrown in our 10 by 10 holding cell, nursing black eyes and bloody noses.

Big Mike looks at me cross the desk.

"Frack and I are taking the remaining prisoners to the jail at the county seat, while you type the report on last night's little donnybrook," he says. "All the data is right there in my notes."

"Me?" I say. "Come on Mike! I'm the one with the goofed up finger."

"You never type with more than two fingers anyway. You'll still have six in reserve."

This is an argument I'm not going to win. Frack gives me an apologetic look, but the boss is the boss.

After they leave with their detainees I check out the cell. The bikers were not big on hygiene. It smells like axel grease and wet dogs. I spray down the cell with Lysol and settle back behind my computer. Mom is in recovery after her last reconstructive surgery, so I put in a call to the hospital before I buckle down to work.

"How did it go?" I ask Dr. Sheldon Firestone, the plastic surgeon who'd come all the way from Madison to work his magic on Gladys's face.

"After she heals she'll look pretty good," he says.

"Will the new face be as good as the one she had before all this happened?"

"Let's wait and see. I've smoothed out some wrinkles, tighten the skin, removed a few more bone chips. If she lays off the cigarettes and booze the work should hold up for the next few years."

Fat chance that's going to happen.

"When can I talk to her?"

"I'd give her about three more hours. She should be fairly lucid by then."

I'm working on last night's report when the mail drops through the slot. It's the usual stuff except for one smudged envelope addressed in pencil to Under-Sheriff Oxenburg, and bearing no return address. It looks personal so I lay it aside.

* * * *

Dyce turns on the coffee maker and jumps into a hot shower. When sunlight shines through the kitchen window and the place smells like strong brewed coffee he knows he's home. He shaves and drinks his first cup. He pulls a plaid snap button shirt from the closet along with a bolo tie with a chunky silver clasp. Jeans. Boots. Hat. He's ready to roll.

He's practiced the heart-felt apology he plans to deliver to Coby until the words don't make sense anymore. He decides to drop the script and play it by ear. He'll know what to say when the time comes.

Dyce is confused when he pulls up to the Dillon place. He didn't expect to see Chili, but he also didn't expect boarded windows and weeds tangled through Miss Amity's rose garden. There were no chickens in the yard. No signs of life. The nearest neighbor came out of his barn, waved at Dyce from across the field and walked over.

"Morning," he said. "You looking to buy?"

"Buy what?"

"The farm." He tugged a For Sale sign out of the bushes and leaned it against the mailbox. "The place went on the market a while back."

"What about the Dillons?"

"Miss Amity is in the Lutheran cemetery and no one knows where the Dillon boy is."

"What do you mean no one knows where he is?"

"Just that. He hasn't been around for quite a spell."

"What about a girl? Long dark hair. French accent."

"She came by a few times but that was a while back."

"Did she ever live with the family?"

"Not that I know of."

"Well, thanks for the information. I appreciate you coming over."

With that the farmer left.

Dyce was confused. This wasn't at all the way he expected things to go.

The next logical stop was Preston's Hardware Store. Maybe the Dillons had moved into town to be closer to the job. He didn't see Coby when he walked into the building, nor had his truck been at the curb. He found Mr.

Preston stacking cans of Wet Patch.

"Good morning, Press," he said.

"Glad to see you back, Dyce. No casts. No broken bones. You must have done okay this season."

"I'm not rich but I'm not in the hole either."

"Well, that's about as good as it gets these days."

"Can you fix me up with a box of rat pellets and five pounds of roofing nails? I gotta do something about my roof."

"Coming right up."

"By the way, when I left, Coby Dillon said you'd hired him on."

"He never showed. Haven't seen him since he applied for the job. Some folks thought he left with you."

"Can't say as he did. Will you let me know if you hear anything?"

"Seems nobody has all summer. Glad to have you back."

Press handed him the bag of nails and the box of rat poison. Dyce paid and left, a slight tremor starting in his bad leg. His hands felt cold and numb. He couldn't believe no one had seen Coby all summer. He drove around town and found it much the same as he'd left it. He picked up only what groceries and cleaning supplies he needed and drove back home.

* * * *

Frack and Mike return to the station in mid-afternoon, Frack carrying a stack of posters bearing the likeness of a bright-eyed young cowboy.

"Here's our boy," says Frack. "Jacob "Coby" Dillon, hometown hero. We found a rodeo program at the Better Business Bureau at the county seat and there was his photo big as life. I've run off 50 copies. By late afternoon we'll have them posted to hell and gone."

"That's great. Let's hope they generate some activity, but you're forgetting one small detail. My finger. Typing is one thing. Swinging a hammertacker is something else. I'll man the phones. You two hang the posters."

"Fair enough," says Mike.

"Yesterday's incident report is on your desk in triplicate and here's your mail." I hand him the letter and he rips it open. He takes out photocopies of three receipts.

"Why would anyone need three old radiators from different makes of car?" he says. "It doesn't make sense and what does it have to do with me?"

"It made sense to whoever sent it," I say.

Frack looks them over. "Hang on a minute," he says, booting up his computer. As soon as he's in, he goes to Explorer and starts tapping away. "Listen to this," he says, reading off the screen.

"Old radiators are used as vapor condensers on illegal whiskey stills. They are lead-soldered and when the lead leaches into the alcohol it is

poisonous. It accumulates in the blood and internal organs of those who drink it. Lead poisoning often mimics the symptoms of other diseases and is known to cause blindness and death. All fittings on a still should be welded or silver-soldered, etcetera, etcetera."

"Someone is trying to tell us something," says Mike.

"While you two hang the posters I'm going to make the rounds of the junkyards," I say. "Where else can you go to find three mismatched radiators?"

"I'll go," says Frack, standing up from the computer. "You should be with Gladys when she comes out of recovery."

"She won't be coherent for at least a couple more hours."

"I say we all go," says Mike. "We'll get the Boy Scouts to hang the dang flyers."

* * * *

Dyce put rat pellets behind the fridge, scrubbed the kitchen and bathroom and changed the linen in both bedrooms, not that he was expecting company. Dusting. Sweeping. Polishing. Done! Everything was fresh and clean by the end of the day. He loaded the fireplace with cedar logs and fists of newspaper but decided to wait for a frigid night before putting a match to it.

No sense wasting fire.

Around ten that evening, when the bars were at capacity, Dyce drove to Gladys's. Even from a distance he could see that something was different. There was only one car in the parking lot and the only light from the interior came from a green beer sign in the window. He parked out front by the totem pole and walked to the entrance. There was a sign on the door that read: Family Emergency. Closed Until Further Notice. Dyce felt the earth shift beneath his feet. Where was everyone? Things were beginning to feel a little otherworldly. He stopped at a liquor store and picked up a twelve pack of beer. He got to the door, paused and returned to the counter.

"Do you carry a liqueur called Mudslide?"

The clerk ran his eyes over the bottles and pulled one off the shelf.

"Here we go."

"What's in it? I've only had it once with a friend."

"Vodka, Kahlua and Irish Cream."

"I'll take it."

When Dyce got home he popped a beer and put a frozen lasagna in the oven. He held the bottle of Mudslide in his hand but didn't open it. He'd save it for a special occasion. He set it front and center on the mantel piece. It would stay unopened, just as the fire would stay unlit.

That night Dyce went to bed with a growing sense of unease.

Coby Dillon.

Gladys's Bar.

The house on Dane Street.

What the hell was going on?

* * * *

The fallen leaves were a thick carpet beneath Brielle's feet as she walked through the woods to the bridge. It was late, sometime after midnight. She watched a full moon float on the surface of the water. There was no one around to notice that she was in her nightgown—no cars, no neighbors, no barking dogs, just the crickets and a sky revolving with stars.

Brielle couldn't sleep. In fact, she hadn't slept well for several nights—tossing—thinking about her life—thinking about Charlie Chereau.

She'd vowed not to come to the bridge again, but that seemed so long ago now. She wasn't the same person she'd been back then, full of mourning and tears. Time had passed, and instead of grieving over what was forever lost, she was looking forward to what might be.

High on Thistle Hill a porch light glowed. Charlie lived alone, but it burned every night like it was waiting for someone to come home. The moon rose higher in the sky, turning from a gold doubloon near the horizon to a silver dime climbing above the treetops. She crossed to the far side of the bridge and walked up the road. She climbed the easy slope of Charlie's driveway and walked up the steps to the porch. If she didn't do it now she never would.

As she stood outside the door she was having second thoughts. What if Suzette was here or some girl she'd never met before. Here she was in her thin white nightgown like a beggar seeking shelter for the night. It could prove embarrassing, but it was a chance she was willing to take. After all, she could never lose what had never been hers.

The door opened as if Charlie had been expecting her. They stood looking at one another in the soft halo of light.

"It's me," she said.

He smiled. "I can see that."

"I'm lonely for you, Charlie. I couldn't wait another day."

"You've always known where to find me," he said, with amusement.

"I wanted to come before but I didn't want to come dragging the past along with me. It took time. I hope you understand that."

"Are you sure this is what you want, Brielle? I'm a pretty average guy compared to a dashing young bullrider, but I can love you and take care of you and give you a warm house in winter."

"You're not average to me, Charlie, not from the beginning and not now. As far back as I can remember, it's always been you."

He led her inside, swept her into his arms and spun her in a circle.

"Now that everyone's home, I guess I can turn off the porch light," he said.

CHAPTER 21

BIG TROUBLE IN LITTLE ABUNDANCE

"There are three commercial sources of old car parts within a 30 mile radius," I say. "Jake's Junkyard, Randy's Wrecks and The Chop Shop. The most likely source is the closest to Frenchman Wood. Gas prices being what they are, people want to drive the shortest distance for what they need. We'll need to pull up a map and do a few calculations."

We're in the process of Googling maps when the front door opens and a thin young man in greasy overalls walks through the door.

"I'm Jonas Philips," he says. "The minute I mailed those receipts I knew it was a dumb move."

"Do come in," says Mike.

"I knew you'd have to hunt down the source. That's what cops do. I work at Randy's Wrecks. The boss would have a fit if he knew I was responsible for police crawling all over his yard, so I decided I'd try steering you in the right direction but remain anonymous."

"Pull up a chair, young man."

"I'll stand if you don't mind. I just crawled out from under a car."

"I'm Mike Oxenburg and these are Deputies Danner and Telusky. So, why don't you tell us what's going on."

"This old crone comes in. She wants a radiator, the third she's purchased from us in the last nine months or so. Doesn't care the make or model, just any old radiator will do. That seemed pretty weird, so when Randy was looking to pull a radiator I start checking out her truck. It's a battered old wreck loaded with moldy hay bales. I peeked between two bales, sort of nudged one aside. I saw a compartment, a wooded frame covered with chicken wire. Underneath were at least a dozen pint jars of clear liquid. I'm sure you can see where this conversation is leading. She was peddling moonshine."

"Sure sounds like it," says Mike.

"A green truck?" I say.

"Yup, green. Heavily oxidized."

"Did you get a name?" asks Frack.

"People like that don't give names. I got the license number though. I didn't see a vin and I doubt it's been registered since the Truman administration."

"Good thinking young man," says Mike. "Thanks for the information. If she comes by again, try to stall her and give us a call."

"I will. I'm on my lunch break. I gotta get back."

Jonas hands Mike a slip of paper with the license number on the back.

"I wasn't here and if you come by the yard you don't know me from Adam, okay? I don't want to get mixed up in this."

Frack peels a twenty from his wallet and hands it to Jonas.

"For making the drive out," he says.

"Thanks man. I can use that."

After Jonas leaves I turn to Frack.

"She's looking more and more like the person who put the bullet in my car door," I say.

"What bullet!" roars Mike. "Why wasn't I told about this?"

The phone rings. I pick it up to avoid Mike's heated stare.

I'm on the phone for 30 seconds when I hang up and shoot out of my chair.

"Gotta go! Gladys suffered a stroke coming out of anesthesia. Frack, tell Mike about the bullet. Really Mike, there's nothing much to tell."

* * * *

When I arrive at the hospital the doctor is back in surgery with another patient. The recovery room nurse ushers me into the room where Gladys lies on a gurney. Her face is swollen from the surgery, the right side of her mouth drawn downward as if by strong gravitational pull. She moans as she struggles toward the edge of consciousness. In addition to the facial reconstruction, her broken teeth have been replaced by dental implants. So much progress, so much courage and now a setback. Two steps forward. One step back.

"We knew a stroke has always been a possibility," says the nurse. "This makes any further cosmetic surgery unlikely, but even without it, she'll look pretty good in six months when the last of the swelling subsides. Here's the good news. They've already Cat Scanned her. This stroke is not a major life-threatening event although we take every stroke, no matter how minor, seriously. She's already on a clot-thinning medication and with therapy she may have no lasting paralysis. We just don't know yet. Best case scenario, she could be released in a week or two."

"That soon?"

"Don't quote me, but it's possible. She'll need rehab, but you can discuss that later with the doctor."

"Mom," I say, squeezing her hand. "It's me, Robely. You're going to be fine."

Gladys attempts to say something. I put my ear next to her mouth.

"What did she say?" asks the nurse when I straighten up.

"She wants her cigarettes."

"People in hell want ice water, but they're not getting it from me."

I bump into Paula in the parking lot. She's picking up a body from the hospital for autopsy.

"How are the men doing from the Summer Camp incident?" I ask.

"They're improving with the help of Chelation therapy."

"Never heard of it."

"It's a synthetic solution that helps remove metals from the body. It won't return them to the condition they were in before the poisoning, but it will hopefully make their lives more tolerable. Anything new on your end?"

"We're following a promising lead. Nothing concrete yet, but I'll keep you posted."

* * * *

A man stands in the wind beside a grave next to the Catholic Church in Frenchman Wood. He's tall and well-built and has the look of a weary old lion who's seen too much of life's disappointments. His hair falls a few inches above the collar of his camel hair overcoat and his short beard and mustache are neatly trimmed. Although his appearance strikes one as rustic and woodsy, he projects an aura of hard-earned success. He wears quality pigskin driving gloves, his car, a Mercedes no more than three years old. He brushes the fallen leaves from the site of his step-daughter's grave and lays a bouquet of white lilies and baby's breath against the stone. It reads, Julie Broussard Chereau.1994-2013. Rest In Peace.

* * * *

A couple days after his arrival, Dyce Dean Jackson drove to the Lumber and Supply in Abundance to pick up roofing materials. When he entered Main Street he felt the air leave his chest. Jacob "Coby" Dillon's face looked at him from flyers fastened to every other telephone pole and taped to half the windows up and down the business district. He had the same disoriented feeling he'd experienced when he'd seen Coby's house boarded up and Gladys's Bar shut down.

He parked along the curb, put on his reading glasses and walked closer to the sign. *Last seen on the evening of Rodeo Sunday, June 4th, 2017.* Dyce felt the color drain from his face. June 4th was the same day of their run-in at Lost Squaw Creek. But, Coby had driven away in his truck. Whatever happened must have happened after he left the bridge. He could think of no other reasonable situation.

Dyce bought the supplies he needed in a trance. If Coby went missing in June, why are the flyers just now being posted? And why only days after Dyce's return to Abundance? One question and a dozen others surface. If Coby is missing where is his truck? Where is the horse trailer? Who put Chili up for auction and when? Coby would never have willingly parted with that horse. She was an expensive animal. At auction she'd only bring pennies on the dollar.

Dyce went back in memory to the night of the storm, how he'd returned to the scene to find the truck and trailer gone and Coby nowhere in sight. He wasn't at his house. He wasn't in the hospital and if Dyce had hit him hard enough to kill him he'd have still been under the tree or in the morgue. If Brielle had found him first, as he'd suspected back then, he wouldn't be missing. If she'd found him dead they wouldn't be looking for him now.

Dyce was sitting on information that was only known to him, information that might be useful to law enforcement. At most, it could help establish a time line, but how could he frame his narrative without becoming suspect number one in Coby's disappearance? He had to give it some serious thought before he made a decision.

* * * *

When I return to the station it's empty and I find a note on my desk. A freezer truck jack-knifed into a ditch between Abundance and Promontory and over a thousand frozen chickens are scattered across the road. Frack and Mike will be occupied for the rest of the afternoon so I man the station and catch up on paperwork.

Frack left the information regarding the green truck on my desk. I'm settling in with the notes when the station door bursts inward and hits the wall, knocking the Out To Lunch sign to the floor. I almost go for my gun until I look up and see a high school boy coming toward me, wide-eyed with fear. I jump out of my chair and meet him half way across the room, gripping his trembling shoulders.

"What's wrong?"

"I'm Alan Clifton. My friend, Joey, is being attacked in The Square. Somebody says he stole Coby Dillon's trophy buckle. They're calling him a killer and punching the crap out of him. Please come!"

I fly past Alan and race down the sidewalk. The town square is down the block and across the street between Main and Cedar. Alan has legs like stilts and blows past me like an Ethiopian. As I cross the street into The Square, dodging a couple honking drivers, I see what looks like a pile-up on a football field.

"Joey's getting squashed under there," cries Alan.

"Sheriff's Department!" I yell. "Break it up! Break it the hell up!"

I grab collars, backpacks and ears, tossing bodies off the stack. Alan is working just as vigorously at my side. An overweight bully, older than the others, is about to nose-dive back onto the huddle when Alan clips him with an elbow and cancels his momentum. He falls back on his butt, howling like a dog, blood dripping from his nose.

We work side by side, thinning out the jumble of arms and legs. My sprained finger gets twisted in a hoody cord. I jerk my finger free and something snaps. Finally we're down to a lone boy lying on the ground, his arms covering his head.

"Everybody get the hell out of here! Go home or I'll throw you all in jail," I say, shaking and breathless from the effort. The crowd scatters in all directions, some of the kids turning to laugh at me or give me the finger.

"He's a murdering piece of trash," shouts a red-faced boy running toward Cedar St.

"Go to hell," shouts Alan at the retreating figure.

Alan and I help his tattered, half-naked friend to his feet.

"He's stealing my buckle," screams Joey, pointing to a disheveled boy taking off across The Square, the buckle dangling from Joey's stolen belt.

"Stop," I shout. "Stop or I'll blow your brains out!" A warning shot isn't even an option but the kid doesn't know that and drops the belt in the grass. "I know who you are, Buzz Barnes, you lazy pimp!"

I admit I'm a little over-wrought. I'm beginning to sound like Gladys. The boy is only fifteen years old. He's not really a pimp that I know of. I don't even know if he's lazy. He's just a bully from the local high school who has a bad attendance record.

"Potty mouth!" he yells over his shoulder when he's at a safe distance. "My parents are going to sue your ass!"

Alan retrieves the belt from the dying grass and hands it to his friend who has tears mixed with dirt and scrapes on his face.

I lean forward gasping for air, my hands on my knees. My finger is turning big and purple. I know what snapped and it wasn't the hoodie cord. As the adrenaline rush subsides the pain hits like a hammer.

"Are you alright," says Joey, as Alan helps him to his feet. He lays a small hand on my shoulder. "Are you having a heart attack?"

"Just catching my breath," I say.

I slowly straighten up and flex my spine. The kid's shirt is gone. The buttons on his fly have flown and he has grass stains on his expensive tan slacks.

"Come along boys. We need to talk."

* * * *

As soon as we arrive at the station I call the mothers of Joey Stern and Alan Clifton. I'm cleaning and applying antiseptic cream to Joey's scratches when the mothers of both boys come through the door. The women are in their late 30's, Mrs. Stern in designer jeans and a gold watch, Mrs. Clifton in overalls with leather work gloves peeking from her back pocket.

There are just enough chairs to seat the gathering.

Everyone is relatively calm as I describe the scuffle in The Square. I offer to call the first responders to further attend to the boy's bruises and scrapes but both mothers and sons decline.

I address the boys. "Would someone like to tell me what started this? First of all, what grade are you in?"

"Ninth," says Joey.

"Joey and I met in advanced math class," says Alan. "Joey's family came out from Boston a month ago. He gets teased at school because he talks like Whitey Bulger and dresses nicer than the other kids."

"So Joey, do you know who Coby Dillon is?"

"I never heard of him until I saw the flyers."

"He's a local rodeo star who's been missing since June. By the time your family arrived in Wisconsin, Coby Dillon had been missing three months so we know that you had nothing to do with Coby's disappearance. The kids that jumped you know that too. They're just being jerks. We're trying to find out what happened to Coby. Right now he's listed as a missing person. We're hoping your buckle might provide a clue. Can you tell me how it came into your possession?"

"Dad helped me buy it at Lucky's Pawn Shop with my birthday money. I thought it was the most beautiful thing I'd ever seen, even nicer than my sister's opal bracelet. Dad said I could start a trophy buckle collection if I wanted to."

"How much did it set you back?"

"One hundred dollars."

Joey unhooks the buckle from the belt. He passes it around so both moms can get a last look at it before it's gone. He places it on my desk without being asked.

I hold the buckle in my hand. It has good weight. It's made of quality sterling silver expertly engraved. "You got good value for your money," I tell the boy. He looks pleased that he's made a good deal.

"It doesn't have a name on it," says Mrs. Stern. "How do you know it belongs to Coby Dillon?"

"It says Abundance Invitational—2017. The bull in the center represents the nature of the competition. There's only one buckle per event so it has to be his. That smooth ribbon shape in the lower right hand corner is where the winner has his name engraved. It's blank."

"You're suggesting he disappeared before he could have his name engraved," says Alan's mom.

"That would be my guess. It's one of the reasons this item could help us in our time line."

"Will I get it back?" asks Joey? "I really love it."

"I don't know yet. If we find Coby Dillon it will have to be returned. In that case I'll see you get your money back."

"How did the pawn shop acquire it?" asks Mrs. Clifton. "And from whom?"

"You have the mind of a detective, Mrs. Clifton. That's going to be my first line of inquiry."

After the boys write a brief statement of the afternoon's events they file out the door with their parents and I go back to the notes Frack left me on the green truck. I'll find time later to write an incident report on the buckle-brawl and make an appointment with the principal of Abundance High. I pick up Mike's notes on the truck and get back to work.

The green truck is a 1955 Chevy pickup. It hasn't been registered since it was stolen from its former owner in 1976. According to the data on the Hall of Records website, the owner of record died in 1989. This is the dead end of all dead ends, unless we're lucky enough to see the vehicle on the road. Who knows? I saw it once. I may see it again. I can't go public or the owner will destroy evidence and we won't get anywhere.

Frack left me a note regarding his background check on Dyce Dean Jackson. Except for a five year old speeding ticket his record is clean.

At the end on my shift I drive back to the hospital. Gladys is sleeping peacefully. I watch her for a while and leave.

It's late when I drag through the gate on Cedar Street. Frack is sitting on the front room sofa with a beer, Fargo sprawled across his lap like a giant bear rug. I go to the fridge and grab a beer for myself. When I return Frack has relocated Fargo to the recliner and I cuddle up next to him—Frack, not the dog. He puts an arm around my waist and pulls me tight to his side. He looks wiped out.

"Get the rig out of the ditch?" I ask.

"We called in a big equipment operator out of Promontory. Took a while but it's done."

"The driver okay?"

"The driver is lucky. Only a bit shaken after taking a couple cartwheels inside the cab. He dozed after 15 hours behind the wheel. You can be sure there'll be an investigation of the labor practices at his trucking company.

"Were you able to salvage the load?"

"In cases like this the insurance provider writes off the whole load. Once the chickens have bounced down the highway they're considered unfit for distribution. We have five good ones in the freezer by the way, and everyone else in town has enough chickens for a month of Sundays."

"So it's not all bad. Wasn't it FDR who promised a chicken in every pot?" I say.

"It was Herbert Hoover in 1928. The market crashed in '29 and for a decade there was nothing in the pot."

"Better late than never."

Frack picks up my hand.

"Ow, ow, ow!" I say. "Don't touch the finger."

"Geezus, Robely! That looks bad." he says.

"I broke it in the buckle-brawl. Every time my heart beats it's like boom, boom, boom!"

"Why don't you fill me in on that?"

He told me his story. I tell him mine.

"I'll hit Lucky's Pawn Shop first thing in the morning," I say.

"After a visit to the doctor," says Frack, firmly.

"Okay, as long as they get me right in. I want to know how Lucky came into possession of a missing man's trophy buckle."

"I'm fading fast," says Frack. "What do we have to eat—other than chicken?"

"Frog legs on ice with shrimp sauce. We can eat in bed and watch the ten o'clock news."

"You really *are* French!" he says, giving me a knuckle rub on the head and making me laugh.

CHAPTER 22

DEMANDING THE TRUTH

When Charlie is busy milling boards for a customer's fence, Brielle takes the truck and drives out to Meadow Road. For the first time since June there are signs of occupancy—the truck in the driveway—Gunpowder in the corral. She walks up the path to the door and knocks.

Dyce opens it and without a word she walks past him into the house. She's wearing new jeans, a tailored suede jacket and a wide turquoise and silver bracelet. A shiny black braid falls over her shoulder. He knows why she's here.

She sits in a chair near the window waiting for Dyce to say something. He takes a chair with the coffee table between them. She looks at him with eyes that are steady and unwavering. She's more mature than when he saw her last. It was a lifetime ago. A different world. She's changed—less trusting—more beautiful—imbued with an unsettling composure. Gone forever is the innocent, spontaneous joy that was her trademark. Today she's all business.

A wedding band on her left hand catches the sunlight.

Dyce is confused.

"You and Coby?" he asks.

She finds his question equally confusing.

"Wherever Coby is, he's not coming back," she said, evenly. "Two nights ago Charlie Chereau and I were married. That doesn't mean I don't owe something to Coby. I want to know what happened to him and what it has to do with you."

"I don't know if I can give you the answer you're looking for."

"Try. Deputy Danner saw you follow Coby from the fairgrounds. Let's start there."

All Dyce can do is look down at his hands.

"You were jealous," she said. It was not a question.

He looks up and meets her unwavering eyes.

"Okay. I concede that point."

"You did what you could to split us up."

"It wouldn't have made any difference. I realize that now."

"You mean he didn't want you in the same way you wanted him. Am I wrong?"

Dyce stared at his boots in silence, choosing his words carefully. "It wasn't like that. He never knew how I felt. For him the partnership was all about rodeo. For me it was family—and more. When he decided to go his own way—well—I had trouble dealing with that."

"What happened? Did you catch up with him in Frenchman Wood?"

He took a deep breath, and favoring his bad leg, rose from the chair. He grabbed his hat and keys.

"Come on. I'm only telling it once and that's going to be in an official capacity."

* * * *

I'm back from the doctor's office with my broken finger in a splint. It was black and swollen. Now it's hot and itchy. I'm ready to drive out to Lucky's Pawn Shop, when a young woman walks in the door with a cowboy straight from central casting. I know from Frack's description that this is the French girl. I recognize the Marlboro Man, Dyce Dean Jackson, from the incident at the Invitational.

I'm alone in the station. Mike's at the Courthouse testifying in a burglary case and Frack's with Animal Control extricating a cow who's stumbled belly-up in a shallow creek bed. Just your typical day in Abundance.

"Come in and have a seat. I'm Deputy Danner."

"I'm Brielle. I spoke with Deputy Telusky at Amity Dillon's gravesite. I was a Broussard then, but now I'm a Chereau."

"Congratulations. I saw your wedding announcement in the weekly. Frank told me about his conversation with you. I turn to Jackson. "So, we meet again, Mister Jackson."

"Yes, ma'am. I'm sorry about what happened that day. I hope you can accept my apology."

"Consider it forgotten. What can I do for you today?" They settle into chairs and I take my place behind the desk.

"I was Coby's rodeo partner for three years," says Dyce. "I was with him the last day he was seen, but I've been on the rodeo circuit and I didn't know he was missing until I saw the flyers. I've come to clear the air and tell you what went down the evening of Rodeo Sunday. It's been eating away at me ever since it happened."

"Ever since what happened? Wait a minute," I say, pulling a small recording device from my desk. "Sheriff Mike and Deputy Telusky will need to hear this as well. I want to make sure your statement is accurately recorded. Any objection?"

"None."

"I press play and record the time, place and names of those present.

"Okay, go ahead, Mr. Jackson."

He speaks fifteen minutes while Brielle sits quietly, intent on every word. I now have his uninterrupted statement regarding the incident at Lost Squaw Bridge.

"Let's make sure I understand this," I say. "Coby promised you another year on the road and changed his mind when he met Brielle. You argued about the dissolution of your partnership. You grabbed his jacket and tore off a couple buttons. He punched your arm and broke your grip. You cold-cocked him and left him unconscious against a tree above the Lost Squaw Creek.

"That's right. I drove off, but my conscience got to me and I went back. When I returned he was gone. A dead man doesn't drive off in a truck pulling a horse trailer. Just to make sure he was okay, I went by his house. He wasn't there. I called the hospital. He wasn't there either. When I couldn't find him I thought he'd connected with Brielle and they'd gone off together as planned. I couldn't contact her because I didn't know her address or phone number. I knew he'd lost a tooth when I punched him, but he was alive when I left him under the tree. I hit the rodeo circuit, and like I said, I didn't find out he was missing until I came back home."

"That's it then?"

"There's more. On my return trip to Abundance I was ten miles outside of town when I saw a girl on a horse I believed was Coby's mare, Chili. I was pulling Gunpowder in the trailer and stopped along the road. The horses recognized one another and started whinnying back and forth. The girl said her dad bought the bay at auction. Coby would never sell that horse and he'd certainly never put her up for auction where he'd only get pennies on the dollar. She was a $10,000 animal. The girl rode up a driveway with a mailbox on the street that said, G. Magneson.

"Thank you, Mr. Jackson." I say. "I appreciate your coming in. When Sheriff Mike listens to the recording, he may have questions or need clarification on some point. I need time to mull this over as well. Can I assume you're not planning a trip to the Outer Hebrides any time soon?"

"I'll be on Meadow Road." He writes down his cell phone number and hands it to me.

"Brielle, where were you when all this was taking place?" I say, letting the machine run.

"Coby and I were going to meet at the bridge. I was going to move in with him at his grandmother's house that evening. I saw him after church before he performed at the rodeo. I can't watch when he rides, so I went home and began packing my things. It was the night of the storm. I got turned around on my way through the woods. We never connected and I never saw him again. Charlie, who is now my husband, found me. When we passed the bridge on the way to Charlie's there was no sign of Coby."

"So, you didn't go back home that night?"

"No, I was too embarrassed. I didn't know if Coby showed or if he changed his mind. I spent the night at Charlie's. We looked for him the next day but couldn't find him."

I click off the machine and write down her cell phone number.

"And your address?" I say.

"We don't have street numbers in The Wood. Take Bridge Road at Paget Corner. My parents, the Broussards, are the last driveway on the right before Lost Squaw Bridge. Charlie and I live up the first driveway beyond the bridge. We're not hard to find once you know where to look."

"Will I hear from you?" asks Brielle. "Coby is still missing. You won't just shelve this and forget about him will you?"

"This case is our first priority. I thank you both for coming in. Please make yourselves available if I need to speak with you again."

I lean back in my chair and watch them leave. Broussard. Starts with B. The Broussard property abuts Lost Squaw Creek where I used to fish and where I left my initials on Grinding Rock. Could Brielle be in some way connected to my long lost father?

I'm way behind schedule. I was expected at the hospital an hour ago. I need to see Lucky about the trophy buckle and someone has to talk to G. Magneson about the horse.

* * * *

I've been visiting with Mom for five minutes when there's a light tap at the door. A man enters wearing a suit, tie and fedora, which means he's either from the big city or doesn't reside in Wisconsin.

"Do you remember me, Miss Calhoun?" he asks, removing his hat like a real gentleman.

"Not really," says Gladys. "I'm not in a remembering mode right now."

"I'm Detective Fred Ferguson, Milwaukee P.D. retired." Gladys's face is blank. "Duane Calhoun? The Margie Downs disappearance?"

"Oh yes, of course. That was a long time ago. How have you been?" she says, her voiced blurred by the stroke but becoming more intelligible by the day.

"Enjoying my retirement. I thought you'd like to know that the disappearance of Margie Downs Calhoun has been solved after all these years."

"You've got to be kidding!"

"I received a courtesy call from Milwaukee P.D two days ago. They knew I'd worked on the case when I was still with the department. An elderly man provided law enforcement with a death bed confession regarding the young lady's murder."

"When did this man die?"

"It's been about five days ago now."

"You've got your wires crossed, Mr. Ferguson. Mr. Calhoun died months ago."

"We're not talking about Mr. Calhoun. We've been focused on the wrong suspect."

"That's impossible!"

"I'm afraid not. She was strangled, and probably sexually assaulted, by her landlord, Mr. Joel Bender, after being abandoned by Mr. Calhoun. Her possessions were not the only things in Mr. Bender's attic. Her mummified remains were discovered in a steamer trunk. Bender was so meek, so starched and ironed, he never became the focus of the investigation. I guess you can't always tell a book by its cover."

Gladys was speechless.

"I wish you a speedy recovery, Miss Calhoun."

"I can't get my head around it," says Gladys, when he was gone. "I was so sure I had it right."

"You want to tell me about it?" I ask, not sure what all this is about.

"No. It was too long ago to matter." Her mood brightens. "Do you realize this means I've only been divorced *three* times? Can you believe it? I'm actually a widow. My marriage to Duane was legal all along, although, it still would have been nice if they'd pinned Margie's murder on him."

"Okay Mom, whatever you say." It was one more eye-rolling moment.

Gladys looks better and grows stronger every day. She can walk a little with assistance or push herself in a walker using one foot. She's frustrated. She's bossy. The nurses can't wait to get rid of her. She'll be released any day I'm told.

Released where? It can't be to the bar. I don't want her at Cedar Street. She'll need a nurse, physical therapy, follow-up appointments. She'll scream bloody murder if I put her in a nursing home. I leave the hospital weighed down by the crush of complicated issues in both my private and professional lives.

After I leave the hospital, I drive to Frenchman Wood, more oriented to the lay of the land this time. I locate the driveway to the Broussard property. I drive across the bridge and see the entrance to the Chereau's. A sign at the bottom of the driveway reads Thistle Mill.

I return to the near side of the bridge and park. I walk along the creek where Dyce and Coby had their altercation. Behind a grove of trees several feet above the water's edge is a sagging cattle wire fence laced through with barbed wire. There are Keep Out signs, some of them broken and lying in the bushes. I look past the fence and see a metal shed, the back of a rundown house and a few sagging outbuildings.

If the last driveway before the bridge leads to the Broussard's house, where is the driveway to this property?

I get on my cell and call the Chereau residence. Brielle answers.

"Brielle, it's Robely Danner. I'm standing on the other side of the creek behind a rundown house. Who lives there?"

"The Rivette's. They're an elderly couple who like to be left alone."

"Where's the driveway?"

"You can't get to it from Bridge Road. You stay on the main highway and turn left on the first logging road past Paget Corner. It's easy to get turned around back there and you may find yourself on the business end of a shotgun."

"While you're behind the place, you need to beware of—"

Brielle didn't get the words out before the fence was rushed by three barking, snarling dogs. I stumble backward and land on my haunch, my heart leaping in my chest. I jump up, embarrassed even though there's no one to witness my graceless tumble. I pick my cell phone off the ground and brush leaf litter from my clothes.

"If you were about to say *dogs*, I just got the message."

"They're scary, but they never jump the fence because of their shock collars."

I thank her for the information and tell her I'll get back to her.

I walk along the creek, then between the road and the back of the Rivettes. I don't see anything that furthers my knowledge of the Coby/Jackson incident. The only leads I have to follow are the trophy buckle and the horse. Whatever happened here has been washed away by wind, rain and the passage of time.

When I arrive back in town the pawn shop is closed. Mike and Frack are back and we listen to the tape together.

"I say Jackson goes to the top of the list," says Mike. "He admits to an altercation that got physical. He may not have thrown the first punch but he was the instigator. We turn our backs and he'll be long gone."

"He came in voluntarily and he owns property in the county. He's not rich and he has nowhere else to go."

"If he bolts it's on you," says Mike.

"Okay, I'll own it," I say, grumpily.

"How do we know Chereau isn't involved in this?" he asks.

"Charlie Chereau? We don't."

"His property abuts the creek. He didn't wait very long before he married the Broussard girl."

"True," I say.

Frack turns to Mike. "How about I drive out to the Magneson place in the morning while Robely has a talk with Lucky at the pawn shop? The horse could turn out to be a good lead."

"I'm good with that," says Mike. "I'll man the phones and keep a lid on things. I'd also like to listen to the tape again and see if there's a pearl mixed in with all those oysters."

* * * *

Anton and Henri keep their newly acquired finds in a pickle jar with their collection of arrowheads, marbles and shell casings. Their buckle money is in a shoe at the back of their closet.

"Tomorrow night we check out the Rivette's shed," said Anton. "It's the dark of the moon, so we're less likely to be seen. We'll bring meat for the dogs."

"It's too risky," said Henri. "Who cares what's in the Rivette's shed?"

"There's a reason for the electricity, like an indoor pot grow. They'd never use unnecessary utilities unless there was money in it."

"You're going to get us killed if you keep this up. We've got the money from the buckle. We should quit while we're ahead."

"Hell, we could get killed crossing the street but it wouldn't be half the fun."

A tapping came from the other side of the wall.

"You boys quiet down so Pete and I can get some sleep!"

"Tomorrow," whispered Anton in Henri's ear. "You'd better not chicken out."

CHAPTER 23

SWINDLED

Frack was familiar with the name George Magneson. Most people were. As a young man George had made his fortune in granite and his quarry was still going strong. He'd agreed to a meeting at the mine office rather than his home.

Magneson was a hands-on boss, directing operations in a hard hat and steel-toed boots. Although he was of average height and build, he looked like he would chew the granite out of the quarry if his men were too slow getting the job done.

Frack walked up to him on the job. "Mr. Magneson, I'm—"

"I know who you are. Frank Telusky the deputy who's shacked up with the lady cop. Us Baptists don't approve of that kind of thing."

"You mean like the Baptist minister in Promontory who drowned his wife so he could be with his pregnant mistress?"

He gave Frack a stony look, then broke into laughter and slapped him on the back.

"I respect a man who gives as good as he gets. Come on in," he said, opening the door to a mobile home that served as his office. "Have a seat." Frack took a chair. George sat across from him at a scarred wooden desk. "Whiskey?"

"A little early for me."

"I expected you sooner. The man who talked to Nancy asked if we'd had Wildflower chipped. The auction house is supposed to do that but this one seems to have slipped by sort of accidently-on-purpose. I took the mare to our vet for a scan and learned the owner of record is the missing man on the poster. Looks like we have a bit of a mystery on our hands."

"Although we have him on the books as a missing person, Coby Dillon has probably been dead since June," said Frack, "so it's unlikely he's the one who put the horse on the block. He paid $10,000 for the animal. It was likely the biggest investment of his life. You mind me asking how much you paid for her?"

"I never buy anything unless I get the best of the deal."

"That horse was Coby Dillon's pride and joy."

"That's exactly how my daughter feels, Deputy Telusky. I, however, have every intention of turning her over to you. I just haven't found a way to break it to Nancy. I suppose the animal will go to the young man's next of kin."

"There is no next of kin, Mr. Magneson. Coby was the last of his line, unmarried and orphaned as a child. I think you should hang onto the horse for now. No need saying anything to your daughter. You bought the animal in good faith, she's obviously well-cared for and your claim of ownership will likely go uncontested. What I need to know is the name of the person who sent the horse to auction."

"The paperwork from the auction house lists the seller as Martha Jones, but you needn't bother running yourself ragged. I've had my lawyer do some checking and he assured me the name is an alias. No such person exists."

* * * *

Lucky's Pawn Shop is in a small converted barn not far from Bubba's Bar. I'm waiting outside when Lucky Fanucci unlocks the doors. It's the one business in town that thrives in hard times, people pawning with great reluctance their guns, musical instruments and family jewelry. Front and center as I follow him inside is a stand supporting an ornate parade saddle flashing rivers of Mexican silver. The $3,000. tag is marked sold.

"A beaut isn't it?" he says. "I found a buyer in 15 minutes on the Internet. A man from Chicago is coming to pick it up later today."

I scan the gun racks behind the counter. "I've never seen so many rifles pawned during deer season."

"Makes the deer happy," he says.

He reaches into a shoe box and lays a form on the counter.

"I heard about the incident with the buckle," he says. "The paperwork is right here."

Fanucci is far too forthcoming. It makes me wonder what he's hiding.

I read: *One hundred dollars received from Joseph Stern, Sr. in full payment for engraved sterling silver trophy buckle.* It's signed and dated by both parties. It appears to be in order.

"Now what I need to see is who pawned the item."

"There wouldn't be a ticket on that. It was purchased outright."

"Then I'll need to see the terms of sale."

"I've already filed away the paperwork on that one."

"Un-file it—please."

"It might take a while."

"Then I'll wait a while."

I hear drawers opening and closing in the small room behind the counter as Lucky kills as much time as he can. He finally reappears with the document in hand, his face flushed.

"Thanks," I say, as he hands it to me.

Belt buckle purchased for $10.00. It was signed by A Bruzard and H. Bruzard, followed by Luca Fanucci's signature and the date.

Bruzard? Any connection to the Broussards?

"It appears that all of the signatures were executed by the same hand," I say. "Why is that?"

"They weren't all that literate. I helped them sign. You know what those people are like back there?

"What people? Back where?"

"Frenchman Wood."

"Are you telling me two individuals were willing to accept five dollars each?

"That's what the paper says."

"They must have been pretty desperate."

"It's the desperate one comes through my door."

"Can you explain how an ordinary belt buckle you paid $10.00 for turned into a sterling silver, hand engraved trophy buckle you sold for $100.00?" A vein throbs in his forehead. "The harder you make me work, Mr. Fanucci, the harder the hammer falls," I say.

"All right. They were minors."

"Illiterate miners digging for gold, or minors, as in under the age of 18?"

"Okay. You got me. They were kids."

"Ages?"

"Eight or nine. Twin boys."

"You're a piece of work Mr. Fanucci."

"They were happy to get the ten bucks."

"Now you can make *me* happy. Give me two fifty dollar bills. I want them clean and crisp."

"Why?"

"To keep this little human interest story out of the newspapers."

The cash register dings and he counts out the cash.

"Thank you. You'll be hearing from me," I say, as I head for the door, all paperwork in hand.

"Wait, just wait a minute! Are you going to turn this into a Federal case?"

"Federal? No, I think the local courts can handle it."

"What if I have information? Something you can use. Maybe you could go easy on me."

I turn around. "It better be good."

"The twins showed me their personal collection of kid-junk. They keep it in a big pickle jar. There were a lot of miscellaneous items: marbles, stones, arrowheads, metal buttons. There was also a chicken bone. They said it kept them safe from the *lupe garu*, a human who takes on the shape of a wolf and sucks the blood out of little kids."

"Sounds a lot like you, Mr. Fanucci."

"Very funny. Anyway, the thing is, it wasn't a chicken bone. It was a human finger, the bone is far too white to be from an Indian gravesite. There was also a tooth, and unless the Fox Indians had gold fillings, I'd say it was contemporary."

"How can I find these boys?"

"Ask around. How many nine year old twin boys can there be in Frenchman Wood?"

"I'll get back with you," I say, pushing out the door.

As I reach the car my cell phone rings. It's the hospital.

"Robely Danner here."

"This is head nurse Nora McAllen. We need you at the hospital, Miss Danner."

"Now?"

"Yes, right away, please."

"Is Gladys all right?"

"Gladys is gone."

"You mean dead?"

"No. The other kind of gone."

* * * *

There are four city cop cars outside the hospital, nurses and orderlies running around in panic mode.

I take the elevator to mom's floor. Nurse McAllen is waiting for me outside Gladys's room.

"Missing? What does that mean?" I say. "She can't even walk unassisted."

"We entered her room forty-five minutes ago and she wasn't in her bed. A wheelchair is also missing. At first we weren't that alarmed, but after a cursory search we called police. So far we haven't been able to locate her."

"I don't understand how this is possible."

"The police are searching every broom closet and bathroom, the staircases, the outdoor landings. Miss Danner, can you think of anyone who might want to help your mother escape?"

"No one comes to mind."

"Anyone who might hold a grudge or try to harm her?"

"I assure you, Miss McAllen, I have an air tight alibi."

* * * *

Back at the station Frack and Mike are at a loss as much as I am. We put out a Senior Alert. We check the bar. Wheezy is alone. I check the house. The doors are locked and Fargo is sleeping under the apple tree. If she's not at the bar or the house, I can't imagine where else she'd be. I wonder if people will be talking about this event 30 years from now. *Remember that feisty old broad who ran the bar? They never found out what became of her.*

I concentrate on work. Frack tells me about his visit with Magneson. It's highly unlikely we'll ever locate the fictitious Martha Jones. I charge my phone and wait for a call that tells me Gladys has been found. It doesn't come. At midnight I'm still awake staring at the ceiling.

CHAPTER 24

THE BOOBY TRAP

Henri chickened out at the last minute. Anton called him a sissy, boxed his ears and made him cry. He then stuffed pillows beneath his blankets to make it look like he was sleeping, just like guys who fool prison guards by putting a wig on a bowling ball.

On his way into the woods Anton picked up the bag of pork chunks he'd hidden in the crotch of a tree, relieved the raccoons hadn't gotten to it first.

There was no moon but the night sky was as clear as a glass bell with stars blazing like bonfires above the trees. Despite the brilliance of the night he was too excited to scratch his mission. Anton jogged through the star-silvered woods toward the Rivette's. The dogs were in his pocket. What could possibly go wrong?

The dogs whimpered and danced at his approach. He was falling in love with those damn dogs. He didn't kick them or zap them with a cattle prod like Sabine did.

Anton slipped cautiously between the wires of the electrified fence, wondering if the old bat could hear the thumping of his heart. He reached the electrical cord twenty feet inside the property line and followed it to the shed.

The screen door opened at the back of the house and Sabine stood silhouetted in the glow of the kitchen light. He flattened himself in the deep shadows against the side of the garage until she went back inside. She could barely see by day so he should be safe under the cover of—well—not complete darkness, but close enough.

There was a lock on the double shed doors facing the house but he made easy entry through the side entrance. He thinks he hears the creaking of the screen door. He stops and listens, decides it's only the sound of leaves scuttling across the tin roof of the shed.

He follows the cord across the dirt floor to where it's plugged into a chest freezer. His shoulders slump with disappointment. No halogen lights. No pot farm. Just a boring old freezer, probably full of poached deer parts, but since he's here he might as well have a look. He tugs at the freezer lid.

It's frozen shut like it hasn't been opened in a coon's age. Whatever is inside has to be gray with freezer burn. He tugs a little harder. This time there's the crunch of ice as the seal lets go. He lifts it an inch and a cold fog as thick as cigarette smoke streams through the crack.

* * * *

Adele rolls toward Pete in the darkness of their room.

"Pete, do you hear that?"

"No. Go back to sleep."

"It's too quiet."

"For heaven's sake, Adele! First the boys are too noisy. Now they're too quiet."

Her mother's intuition is seldom wrong, especially when it comes to the twins.

Adele walked down the hall to the boy's room and snapped on the bedside lamp. Henri sat up and blinked. She kissed him on the cheek.

"Go back to sleep," she said.

She touched the soft lumps on Anton's bed and discovered pillows arranged in the shape of a boy.

"Pete, get in here! Anton is gone."

Unable to keep his brother's secret under Adele's withering gaze, Henri began to cry.

* * * *

When the phone rings this late, Brielle knows something is wrong. She listens to her mother, hangs up and calls for Charlie.

"Anton is on his way to break into the Rivette's."

Charlie grabs his shotgun from the rack. As he cuts cross-country toward the bridge Brielle puts in a call to Deputy Danner.

Within 60 seconds, our guns are in our shoulder holsters our badges clipped to our belts. Frack and I race over the deserted highway, sirens blaring, light bar flashing red and blue into the trees along the road. We skid onto Bridge Road. Even with good suspension, the car bottoms out on the ruts. I know there's another way to the Rivettes, but I can't risk getting lost in uncharted territory. We'll have to gain entry through the back and that means dealing with the dogs.

* * * *

Anton carefully lifts the lid of the freezer and the dim light inside flicks on. Inches of frost-fluff have collected below the cover. He brushes the frosty covering away with his hand. It's solid beneath the snow, as if someone had filled the interior with water and let it freeze over. There's something buried in the ice but it's too cloudy to make out a form. He brushes away a few more inches of frost and an object begins to take form. It's something big, filling all of the useable space.

Anton bends over and peers deep into the freezer his eye almost touching the ice, expecting to find large sides of venison or a few braces of pheasant. Instead, two frozen human eyes look directly into his, eyes filled with horror and surprise, just as they were at the moment of his death. His mouth is agape, his last scream frozen in his throat. There's a rope twisted tightly around his neck.

Anton shrieks and stumbles backward. He wants to run home and pretend he was never here, that he never saw what he saw, that his eyes were playing tricks.

As Frack and I run through the trees, we see Charlie disable the electrified fence, pull up the post and toss it aside. He crosses onto Rivette land without waiting for us to catch up. The dogs scatter at the sight of his shotgun and dive beneath the porch.

The side door opens silently behind Anton. The pale freezer light casts a dim glow around the shed. He turns around at the sound of boots scraping the ground and looks into Sabine Rivette's half-seeing, ice-water eyes. The shotgun at her hip shifts in his direction.

"No!" he screams. "It's just me, Anton."

At the sound of his voice she adjusts her aim until it's dead on.

"Don't!" he cries. "I'm just a kid."

"A Broussard!" she replies. "A thieving little Broussard!"

Anton makes a run for the double doors at the front of the shed, hoping to push through the space where the two doors meet at the center. Running full speed in the semi-darkness he hits a roll of barbwire stretching from one side of the shed to the other, a booby trap strung with cowbells and tin cans. It makes a terrible racket.

He thrashes wildly but only gets more entangled, the sharp barbs biting into his clothes and skin. He screams his head off like a little girl, remembering with regret how cavalierly he'd called Henri a sissy and realizing too late that his brother was smart enough to pull out of the ill-conceived heist.

Just as the old woman twitches her finger on the trigger she drops like a stone, the butt of Charlie's gun tapping her sharply on the back of the head. He catches her shotgun as it falls and sets both guns against the wall. He approaches Anton and begins untangling him from the booby trap.

"Stop screaming," says Charlie. "You'll wake the dead."

Anton's eyes are wide with terror.

"I won't wake the one in the freezer," he says.

Charlie's hands stop working the wire.

"What did you say?"

By the time Frack and I enter the shed, Brielle is running across the bridge, and a man I assume is either Paul Bunyon or another Broussard, emerges, armed, from the woods. The redbones, realizing they're not being gunned for after all, crawl from beneath the porch and surround Anton with whines and kisses as he's finally released from the booby trap.

Charlie levels Anton with a hard look.

"The next fix you get into, you better be man enough to get out of it by yourself."

Frack bends over Sabine and feels a pulse in her throat. He calls for an ambulance.

I shine my flashlight around the shed and walk deeper into the back of the building past the farm equipment and non-op cars, not realizing the main event is in the freezer. Near the back wall is an old green truck with hay bales in the back. It's parked beside Coby Dillon's newer white truck. I don't see the horse trailer and imagine it's already been sold.

Frack motions me over to the freezer.

"Brace yourself," he says. "It's bad."

I look inside thinking I'm prepared for what I'm about to see, but the eyes staring up at me are not those of Coby Dillon, but of an elderly murder victim. Cops are not supposed to faint—and I don't—but I've never come this close before.

Charlie walks over.

"Do you recognize this man?" asks Frack.

He looks inside the freezer.

"That's old Devil Rivette. I guess he's sicker than we thought."

"That's Coby Dillon's truck back there," I say. "If this is Rivette, where the hell is Coby Dillon?"

"I wouldn't have any thoughts on that," says Charlie. "You're the detective Miss Danner."

Frack leaves to check the perimeter of the buildings.

"The ground on the Rivette property is peppered with buckshot," he says, when he returns. He glances once more into the freezer, then over at the old woman crumpled on the floor.

"I think we've just been introduced to Martha Jones, the woman who put Coby's horse up for auction," he says. "I believe what happened to Coby happened somewhere on or near this property."

The man we saw walking out of the woods takes charge of the boy.

"Stop sniveling like a baby," he says. "You went looking for trouble and you found it."

"This is Pete Broussard," says Charlie, "and this young troublemaker is his son, Anton." Anton wipes away a tear and looks at his feet, not half so brave as he was when he first walked into the woods.

"Pleased to meet you, Pete," I say.

"Ma'am. You going to take this boy in?"

"Right now I have bigger fish to fry. How about we place him in your custody."

"Thank you. There will be consequences."

This is my partner, Frank Telusky," I say. "We need to stop by your house on our way back to the station. Your boys may hold the key to a mystery we're trying to solve."

"We'll be waiting."

Pete walks over and looks inside the freezer.

"About what I expected," he says.

"Everybody out," says Frack. "We need to preserve the scene for the M.E." As he clears the area, I'm dialing Paula's home phone.

* * * *

Charlie and Brielle walk back over the bridge, his arm protectively around her shoulders. I'll never know how things might have worked out between her and Coby. Who knows? They might have lived happily ever after, but as I watch her walk away beside Charlie Chereau, I feel they couldn't be a better match.

Pete leaves with Anton at his side and disappears into the trees followed by the Rivette's redbone hounds.

The ambulance wails in the distance.

* * * *

The pickle jar proves to be a treasure trove of circumstantial evidence. The tooth and the human finger bone go to the lab for identification. The heel is from a cowboy boot of the brand Coby wore and a search deep in the woods unearths a skull with one tooth missing, a scattering of human bones from the forest floor and fragments of denim and leather matching the clothes the young man was last seen wearing. The bones and remnants of clothing were heavily pocked with buckshot, making clear the cause of death.

We speculate that Coby, returning to consciousness and somewhat disoriented got turned around in the storm and wandered toward the Rivette's back fence instead of the road. He was shot by Sabine Rivette, thinking in her paranoia, that he was another thieving Broussard. She managed to drag his lifeless body deep into the woods, probably with the help of party or parties unknown. She certainly had no help from Devil because he was already dead. She couldn't hide Coby in the freezer because her husband already occupied that space.

She admits strangling Devil when he was too sick to manage the stills.

Between him, the stills and the dogs, something had to go and caring for Devil took the most effort. Due to dementia from ingesting her own contaminated liquor, Sabine will probably spend the rest of her life in a care facility or the hospital unit of a prison. One day soon the old feud will be laid to rest with the silence of her bones—Sabine—the last surviving Rivette.

I give Pete Broussard the two $50.00 bills the twins have coming from the true value of the buckle. The buckle itself was returned to the Stern boy.

* * * *

On an icy morning in early November I visit the gravesite where Jacob "Coby" Dillon is buried beside his grandmother. His only sin was the misfortune of being at the wrong place at the wrong time. I lay flowers by the stone. Frack and Mike and I have given our hometown hero the only gift we had to give. We solved his murder. We did our job.

When I get back to my desk I call Brielle Chereau and Dyce Dean Jackson and ask them to come by the station. I'd held back the metal buttons from the pickle jar and I set them on the desk in front of us.

Tears immediately well in Dyce's eyes.

As Brielle looks at the buttons I see no sign of recognition on her face.

"Do you know what these are?" I ask.

"They're the buttons I ripped off Coby's denim jacket," says Dyce.

"Do either of you know what words are stamped into the metal?"

Brielle shakes her head.

"I can't read the words without my glasses," says Dyce, "but they say, Cabelas. Since 1961. It's the name of Coby's favorite Western store."

Brielle looks into Dyce's face and any animosity she once harbored is gone. She slowly slides the buttons off the desk into her hand. She turns to Dyce, presses them into his palm and closes his fingers around them.

"Coby would want you to have these," she says. She rises from the chair and walks through the autumn rain to the truck where Charlie waits.

CHAPTER 25

THE LONG ROAD HOME

Dyce left the substation for the last time and drove home through the first major storm of the season, two metal buttons tucked inside his wallet. Rain came down cold and hard, ripping the last dead leaves from the trees. Snow was predicted before the night was out.

He parked the truck and ran through the rain to the door. Once inside he hung his jacket on the hall tree and pulled off his boots. He started toward the kitchen and stopped short. In front of the hearth was a duffle bag with a saw and level sticking out the top. A pair of black and turquoise boots leaning against a back pack sent a pleasant shock through Dyce's heart.

Kai Furlong stirred in the recliner. Sleepy-eyed, he pushed a rebellious lock of blonde hair out of his eyes.

"Kai!" One word. A joyful outburst.

He didn't wonder how Kai gained entry because no one around Abundance bothered locking doors.

"Came to thank you for the boots," he said, climbing stiffly out of the chair. "Nobody ever gave me anything that nice in my whole life."

"My god, it's great to see you!" They bumped fists and crushed one another in a bear hug.

"I saw the bottle of Mudslide," said Kai, stepping back so he could read Dyce's face. "It freaked me out, man, almost like you were expecting me."

It was true. Kai was always there in the back of Dyce's mind whether he was grooming his horse or polishing his boots, a long shot more than an expectation.

"I imagine the news about your aunt isn't good," said Dyce.

"She's gone. When the farm went it took her with it. A person can only take so much loss in one lifetime. Bank took the cows and the farm equipment. Only thing they left behind was the dust."

Dyce grabbed Kai and held him at arm's length. "How the hell did you get here?"

"The engine blew my first day on the road and I hitch-hiked the rest of the way. Dragged my tools along, being they're the last of my worldly possessions. All I can say is, you want me gone, don't let me get settled in. I can turn into a tumbleweed and blow on down the road. I can also swing a mean hammer and fix your roof. You may not have noticed but there's a leak above the kitchen sink."

"You must be starved," said Dyce. "I can count your bones through the skin." He went to the kitchen, made coffee and threw together a plate of sandwiches. They sat around the kitchen table catching up on things, listening to the roof leak drop by drop into the sink.

"How do you feel about we get a t.v. and order cable?" said Dyce. "I've been thinking about it a long time but it's no fun unless there's someone to watch it with. Football? Homicide Hunter? Old movies? What do you say?"

"Does that mean I can stay?"

Dyce grew serious for a moment.

"I got nobody else in this whole wide world. You're it kid."

"You can't be more alone than I am," said Kai, with a crooked grin. "I say yes to the t.v."

"We are so damn pathetic," said Dyce and they burst out laughing.

"Then it's settled. Just one question."

"Shoot."

"Did Smoky cough up the hundred dollars?"

"Hell yes! He gave me a party and everybody came. Darlene sends her love and Barbie Fuller says she'll catch you the next time around."

They broke into peals of laughter and spent the rest of the afternoon smoking cigarettes, playing cards and deciding what size flat screen would look best above the mantel.

That night they settled in front of the fireplace—Dyce, Kai and the bottle of Mudslide. Fire crackled on the grate, wind rattled the windows and sent a shudder through the bones of the old house.

"I know things other people don't know," said Kai.

Here we go again, thought Dyce.

"And what would that be?"

"I can look into that fire I see us walking together to the end of that long, dusty road."

And they did.

Jimmie Dean and the Marlboro Man.

* * * *

Every time the phone rings we hope it's news of Gladys telling us she's been found safe, but the call never comes and we have no leads to follow. Too much time has passed. She's elderly. She's not well. We begin to lose hope. The rain is coming down and Fargo is snoring softly in the bed between us when the phone rings. Caller I.D. says it's coming from Gladys's

Bar. We don't want to answer but we do. It's Wheezy.

"I need you at the bar," he says breathlessly. "Something's come up. I can't talk about it on the phone."

"An emergency?" I ask.

"Depends on how you look at it."

It wasn't like Wheezy to be evasive, but if it was a dire emergency he'd have said so.

"I'll be right down," I say.

"Not by yourself," says Frack. "There are still three ex-husbands out there somewhere."

We laugh

We pull on jeans and strap our shoulder holsters over the top of our thick winter sweaters. Within minutes we pull into the lot in front of the totem pole. The lights in the bar are turned low. We hear laughter coming from inside and see an expensive car in the lot. I doubt it belongs to anyone we know.

"What's going on?" I say.

"Guess we'll have to go in and find out."

We walk inside together to find Gladys sitting in the hospital wheel-chair with a beer in her hand and a cigarette planted on the good side of her mouth. Except for the swelling her face resembles the one I remember.

"Mom! What the hell is going on?" I'm torn between relief and anger. "You've got the whole county looking for you."

"Oh please!" She waves her cigarette at me. "Don't be such an alarmist. You have no idea how boring it gets in the hospital. You can't get better in a place like that."

"Well, how—?"

She motions toward the bar where someone stands in shadow.

"He's the one rode to my rescue," she says. "We spent some time with his family up on Bridge Road."

Bridge Road? My head is spinning.

"What are you talking about?"

"They finally let bygones be bygones," she says. "Why the hell not? It's been almost 30 years."

My heart is beating faster as the pieces of a very old puzzle begin to fall into place.

"He's staying long enough to get me to my first physical therapy appointment. Then he's going home. He has a lumber yard in British Columbia. I have a bar in Abundance. Neither one of us are going anywhere so don't go reading something into it."

The mystery man standing in the shadows behind the spigots walks around the edge of the bar into the light. He stops half way across the floor.

I stand frozen. I can't take my eyes off of him. He bears a striking resemblance to Pete and a familial, but lesser resemblance to Charlie Chereau. Rugged. Woodsy. There's another layer to him as well, something more worldly and refined.

"I'm turning in," says Gladys, irritably. "Frack, wheel me into my new room. I can't do the stairs yet. There. The door to the left of the bar."

I barely notice as she's wheeled away, but I hear her cigarette cough as Frack gets her settled in.

Suddenly I'm all alone in the bar, Frack and Wheezy gone up to the second floor.

The stranger looks at the splint on my finger and a slight smile appears on his lips.

"Looks like you take after your father," he says.

I fly across the room into his arms. Silent tears run down my cheeks. I don't have to look at his hand to know this is my father. It's the first time since I was three or four that I've felt those familiar arms around me. I step back. I take his left hand and press it to my cheek. He still has the woodsy scent of pine and wood smoke in his clothes, wears jeans and a Pendleton shirt just like I remember. He was the first person in my life who wanted me, but Gladys would have me, simply so he couldn't.

"I've been looking for you my whole life," I say. "I've pulled up every public record I could think of. It's not easy when you don't have a name, only a line on a Birth Certificate with *father unknown* typed in. I knew it wasn't true. I remembered."

He smiles. "You should have looked on the deed to the bar. Gladys and I are joint tenants. Have been since before you were born. I'm half owner but I don't get involved in her business. I guess you could call me the silent— and absent—partner."

"You look like a Broussard," I say, not yet certain I have it right.

"Robert Louis Broussard."

I take a moment to let it sink in. R. B.

"Brielle is your cousin. Her father Pete is my younger brother. The twins, of course, are your cousins too, although I can't imagine anyone wanting to claim them." We both smile. "Henri is getting his pony. Anton will have to wait another year as punishment for his disobedience, but Pete is allowing him to keep the redbone hounds. They have to go somewhere."

I feel complete for the first time since I was very small and my father was in my life.

"Robely, after Robert," I say. "I've always loved my name. Dance with me, Dad. Something slow."

"Do we need that gun between us?" he says, with a smile.

I unbuckle the holster and thump the rig onto the bar.

"Your choice," he says, looking at the juke box bubbling away in the corner.

I drop a quarter in the slot and push K7. Freddie Fender drops on the turn table.

My father takes me in his arms and I rest my head on his shoulder.

I want to say, *don't ever leave,* but that's not going to happen. He has his life and I have mine, but he'll always be my father and I'll always be his daughter. No one can take that away from us. R. B. Robely Broussard. The mystery of Grinding Rock is solved.

As we dance, rain turns to snow outside the window. The record spins. The needle drops.

> *If you're ever feeling blue,*
> *Remember I love you.*
> *I'll be there before the next teardrop falls...*

www.ingramcontent.com/pod-product-compliance
Lightning Source LLC
Chambersburg PA
CBHW020146180626
46810CB00004B/1749